The Captive
in the Tale

The Captive
in the Tale

K.J. STEWART

Library of Congress Control Number:		2019900695
ISBN:	Hardcover	978-1-9845-0520-0
	Softcover	978-1-9845-0519-4
	eBook	978-1-9845-0518-7

Print information available on the last page.

Rev. date: 01/19/2018

To order additional copies of this book, contact:
Xlibris
1-800-455-039
www.Xlibris.com.au
Orders@Xlibris.com.au
775580

Whatever is done for love always occurs beyond good and evil.
— Friedrich Nietzsche

PROLOGUE

A NEBULOUS BLANKET CLOAKED THE trail, muffling the man's footsteps. Just as well. His was a covert mission, secret men's business. He felt powerful even while he suppressed a groan, the muscles in his shoulder burning under their load.

Slivers of wan moonlight pierced the forest canopy, and the man pushed aside a branch with his forearm. He ducked to avoid a twig that snapped back, narrowly missing his cheek.

He paused, breath laboured. While he rested, he glanced at the weight dangling against his hip. A wisp of hair had escaped its plastic casing, the colour reminding him of the dirty sand of a child's playground.

A glance skyward confirmed the approach of daybreak, and the man hoisted it over his shoulder, grunting as he set off again. His plastic-coated shoes rustled along the track strewn with debris and protruding obstacles. As much as he wished to hurry, it wouldn't do to trip and dislodge his load. He'd studied the skills of a hunter, the most important being to never leave a trace. It was a lesson well-learned.

Another two hundred metres, and the man found what he had sought. The trail widened, an ancient gum tree standing at the deepest point of the arc. It was the perfect backdrop to display a hunter's trophy.

His arms and spine strained as he tilted to one side, letting the weight slip from his grasp. It landed at the base of the massive trunk, head lolling.

The man rummaged through his jacket pockets, organising their contents on a sheet of painter's plastic he had laid on the ground. There was a knife, a length of thick rope, nails of pockmarked iron, and a hammer.

The man cut away the outer sheathing, moaning as he manoeuvred the package into position. He wound the rope around it, tugging at the plaited twine before knotting it at the rear of the trunk. A grim smile creased his sallow cheeks as he viewed his handiwork.

He sucked in the frigid air through his nostrils, exhaling a puff of steam. With clenched fists, he beat his chest, his breath now coming in pants. He clapped his hands and reached for the nails and hammer. With a final glance, he grasped an arm and lifted it high until it rested against the smooth bark. He shifted and placed the tip of a spike against its pale surface.

With a low roar, the man swung the mallet, the noise of clanging metal ringing through the predawn. He closed his ears to the sound of cracking bone and swung a second time. The iron point thudded and embedded in the thick bark. Once he'd tested the spike to make sure it held, he proceeded to the other side, where he repeated the process.

The man fought the wave of nausea crashing against the walls of his stomach. He bent at the waist, counting his breath until it abated. He'd vomited the first time, burrowing his head into a plastic bag so as not to splatter the ground or leaves with his DNA-infused mess.

Satisfied he'd secured the prize, he fussed around it. The crown slumped forward, and he plucked a hairbrush from his top pocket and sank to his haunches. With clumsy strokes, he ran the brush through its matted locks until they untangled into a glistening sheet. Next, he smeared gloss across full lips and hitched up the hem of the red dress. Before he finished, he pulled out a phone and snapped several shots from different angles.

As he retraced his steps along the path, the man's shoulders sagged, his features softening the farther he got from the trophy now on display.

Behind the wheel of his van, he pursed his lips and whistled the theme song to *The Muppet Show*. When his vehicle joined the early-morning drivers navigating the winding mountain road, his mind focused ahead. He was going home, and his face split into a wide grin, flashing an uneven row of chipped and tobacco-stained teeth.

CHAPTER 1

For Gina Palumbo, the day started like any other. She woke up in her apartment and shrugged into running clothes before going through her warm-up ritual. Her movements were stealthy, the bedroom cloaked in darkness so as not to wake her girlfriend, Tara. Sunlight peeked through the blinds as she slipped into the building's hallway. She never took the lift, preferring instead to take the five flights of stairs onto the street.

She walked across the road separating the apartment block from the Pacific Ocean. The sun shimmered across the water, spraying golden the crest of rippling waves. Life was good, she conceded as she bent forward to clasp her ankles, stretching through her calves. She felt strong as she took off, her pace easy along the slope leading onto Bondi Beach.

After the smooth asphalt, the sand snatched at her ankles, and her feet churned, sending the grains scattering. When she reached the firm surface where the waves lapped at the shore, she breathed, settling into a steady rhythm. Time became measured by the drumming of her sand shoes and her pounding heart.

Gina had always been active, the shelves of her childhood room displaying the spoils of her victories. There were medals for athletic and swimming carnivals, as well as trophies for various school teams. Her prowess helped her survive a difficult adolescence. She'd channelled her frustration and confusion into it, drenching her 'unnatural' thoughts in the sweat of exertion. It became a disguise for her, a way to hide the freak who fantasised about nuzzling into Pamela Tyson's long curls.

Back at the apartment, Gina stripped off her sweaty clothes and stepped under a stream of tepid water. Her head hung forward, rivulets running through her hair. She screwed her eyes shut and bent double, palms against the wall tiles propping her up while she rotated the hot tap until the gushing torrent scorched her flesh-covered spine.

Behind Gina's eyelids, images rushed at her in vivid Technicolor. A phantom whiff of eucalyptus assailed her nostrils, at once returning her to the crime scene in bushland at the base of the Blue Mountains.

She and her partner had been investigating the disappearance of a Sydney woman when their sergeant reported the discovery of a body at Glenbrook matching her description. A pair of locals had found her during their morning walk, and by the time the officers arrived, forensics was working the site.

Spikes through her wrists pinned the woman to the trunk of a gum tree. Her torso slumped forward, hair veiling her face. Gina had crouched by the kneeling body and swept the golden locks to one side. She'd recognised Jenna from the photos her husband had provided them that morning.

When she and Ravinder returned to the station, she'd headed straight to Detective Inspector Munce's office. The crime scene bothered her, the way the killer had staged it, every detail significant in ways she didn't yet understand. Whatever his motives and psychosis, she was sure he was just getting started.

Munce had advised her to stick to the facts. They had a single murder, albeit a macabre one, committed by an unknown perpetrator. As much as she trusted her intuition, Gina wasn't confident enough yet in her new position to labour the point.

Five years had passed since 'the Sylvia incident', their name for what transpired in the mountain village of Leura. Gina always capitalised it in her mind, the time she had spent with the daughter of a serial killer.

During the ensuing years, she'd learned the bones of police work on the streets of Sydney, its highs and lows, pressures and obstacles. She'd known failure and mistakes, learning from each to become a better officer.

While she and Munce had forged a friendship based on mutual respect, he'd shown her no quarter. If anything, he was harder on her than the other probationary constables or probies, as seasoned officers called them. When she'd discarded her P-plates, he announced that he expected her to reach the rank of detective constable within five years. She hadn't disappointed him, earning her credentials after four and a half.

'Akeisha and Bec will be another ten minutes.' Tara's voice reached through the glass screen, bringing Gina upright. For a second, she swayed on her feet, the return to the present triggering a bout of dizziness.

She twisted the shower taps, flesh prickling as the frigid air penetrated the lingering steam. When she opened the glass door, Tara held out a towel, which she clasped against her body.

'Did you hear me?' Tara asked with a raised eyebrow.

Gina grunted, her mind lingering on the murder investigation. She recognised today was special, but she couldn't shake the thought that Jenna Jacklin's killer was at the beginning of his 'career'. It drummed against her mind no matter how hard she tried to block it.

'They're here!' Tara called out five minutes later while Gina shrugged into a blue-and-white striped blazer and smoothed it over fitted black pants.

A second later, the doorbell rang, and she shook her head, lips twitching. She didn't know how Tara did it, but she had a habit of announcing visitors before the bell heralded their arrival.

She stepped into the living room to find Tara caught in the embrace of their closest friends, Bec and Akeisha. They'd made the trip from Leura, a village sitting near the top of the Blue Mountains. Known for its rugged landscape, quaint shops, and resplendent gardens, it had also gained unwelcome notoriety after the Sylvia incident.

'Get in here!' Bec called, one hand waving to her.

As Gina joined the group hug, she felt her mind shift, shutting against thoughts of murdered women. Today was for celebration and joy, not corpses.

CHAPTER 2

THE BREEZE CARRIED THE smell of the sea – salt and seaweed – as Gina drank in the endless blue expanse of the Pacific Ocean. No matter how long she'd lived in Bondi, she never tired of the ever-shifting sea – the ripples of the morning replaced now by tumbling water churned a murky green.

Bubbles made her nose twitch as she leaned her elbows atop the wall enclosing the rooftop terrace, sipping from a champagne flute. She pivoted when she heard her name called.

'George is here!' Tara yelled from the stairwell door.

Gina raised her glass in greeting. Dressed in civilian attire, Munce still appeared to be in uniform. Today he'd chosen tan pants, a maroon-coloured Ralph Lauren polo, and brown dress shoes buffed to match the belt cinching his waist.

His wife, Harriet, wore her usual composed mask. In her fifties, her impeccable grooming always left Gina feeling unkempt. Her discomfort extended beyond the older woman's external visage to her inscrutable expression. Polite to a fault, she contributed to discussions with insight and wit, even laughing at Gina and her friends' lame jokes. Still, the younger woman detected an undercurrent of stoicism beneath her demeanour.

She accepted Harriet's dry peck before turning to Munce, who beamed and embraced her. 'Congratulations,' he said as they pulled apart, eyes moving between her and Tara.

'Thanks, George,' the latter replied with a lopsided grin, arm snaking around her girlfriend's waist.

'Yes, thank you, sir.' Gina emphasised the last, causing Tara to snort and chortle in one blast of noise. She enjoyed flaunting the casual way she addressed the senior officer.

Gina scanned the gathering before spying a cluster of colleagues. *Typical cops*, she thought with a wry smile, their eyes roving the civilian crowd for any perceived threat or wrongdoing. She guided George and Harriet toward them, grinning when they stood to attention. One or two had to stop themselves from saluting.

'At ease, gentlemen, ladies,' Munce ordered with mock severity, defusing the tension.

The group returned to discussing the latest round of probies. Their short memories never ceased to amaze Gina. She remembered the first months on the job: anxiety about stuffing up, the humiliation and reprimands that followed when she did. It had kept her from joining in; now the shoe was on the other foot.

Her friend, Sinead, interrupted her musings. 'I was sent to tell you it's speech time,' she whispered, causing her to cringe.

Tara stood beside the stereo, and Gina spotted her father heading to join her. His florid face and the half glass of raki in his hand elicited a groan from her. *Great*, she thought. She squared her shoulders and navigated the crowd to take her place between the pair.

Her girlfriend grabbed her hand and squeezed. They exchanged a smile, and for a moment, Gina forgot where they were, leaning forward to brush her lips across Tara's. Clapping and whooping jolted her back to reality. She flushed while Tara laughed unselfconsciously in a way she envied.

She didn't notice her father move until a tapping noise replaced the saccharine strains of Indie artist, Julia Jacklin.

Anastasios spoke, lips against the microphone so his words came out as incoherent mumbling.

Gina stepped forward. 'Hold it away, Papa,' she instructed, pulling the microphone from his face. 'There. Now try.'

'Test . . . I am testing this,' Anastasios said with a beam as laughter rippled through the crowd. 'Hello and good afternoon,' he continued, shifting the microphone to drain his glass in one gulp. 'Here,' he said, swivelling to face Gina, 'you take.'

'I won't talk long,' he said after she'd done as he ordered. 'But I have things to say, and it will take as long as it takes, okay?'

Gina grimaced and shook her head while Tara snorted beside her.

'Eugenia was a sweet girl,' her father continued, 'but caused mischief just the same. Oh yes, she did,' he added when someone voiced their mock surprise. 'Even when little, when her dear mama was alive . . .' Anastasios broke off, dropping his head. He wiped his sleeve across his face and lifted his gaze. 'Me and Stephania, we sit on lounge after Eugenia go to bed. From nowhere, a . . . how you say . . . *orsacchiotto?*'

'Teddy bear!' his eldest daughter, Leda, called from the throng.

'Yes, yes,' Anastasios mumbled before his face split into a wide grin. 'This bear, it fly in air and land on the floor near me and Stephania.'

He paused and glanced at Gina, who smiled. She loved this story.

'My wife, she ask, "Why you throw bear? I thought you love him." It turns out little Eugenia was making test for us. If she throw bear and he get in trouble, she run to bed quick smart. If bear get no trouble, she sneak into room behind couch. Even young, she make good under-the-cover police.'

While laughter erupted, Gina groaned through her grin. Here she was, worrying about her father speaking. Now she wondered how to follow him.

'Eugenia is my baby, youngest of three beautiful girls,' Anastasios continued, dipping his head toward Gina's sisters. 'She was strong but in quiet way so you don't know you give her what she want.' He tapped one finger to the side of his nose and grinned. 'Her mother say, "This one will be fine. She knows who she is without having to shout to world." She was smart lady, my Stephania.'

Anastasios cleared his throat. 'She would be proud today, proud always, of her girl. She is fine woman,' he continued, gesturing for Gina and Tara to join him. 'And she marry fine woman too. Me, I am old-fashioned. There is a lot I don't understand in modern world, like computer and these smarty-pant phones. But,' he continued above the smattering of laughter, 'love, I know, and these young people have plenty. I could not ask for better…' He turned to Gina and Tara. 'Will she be wife, both wives?'

Gina nodded without speaking while Tara beamed and reached to pat his hand. 'That's right, wife and wife.'

Anastasios raised his arms. 'See? Still much, I don't understand. But I try. Now enough from an old man. Where's my drink?' He swivelled his head until someone placed a full glass in his hand. 'There now. I ask you good people to raise your glass to Eugenia and Tara. I hope you are happy, same as me and your mother.'

Amid thunderous applause, Gina's father embraced her, his cheeks damp with tears. Her own melted into his while he drew Tara into the hug. When they pulled apart, the three of them giggled, mopping their faces.

Tara stood on tiptoes and planted a kiss on Anastasios's cheeks, while he blushed and chortled. She took the microphone from his hand. 'Lucky me, going on after the top billing,' she announced. 'Oh well, here goes.'

'When I met this stunning woman,' she continued, glancing at Gina with a smirk, 'she was shy, awkward. Luckily, I'm neither.' Tara grinned when their friends yelled their approval. 'Gina didn't give much of herself, and it would have been easy to allow her to push me away, but . . . Well, I'm not one to take the easy road.' She broke off with a snort. 'Back then, I couldn't guess at her kindness, intelligence, and compassion, and yet I haven't uncovered half of this amazing being. So here is my pledge to you.' She grasped Gina by the shoulders. 'I will treat every day as a grand adventure and will never shun a single facet of yourself you wish to unveil. There's no part I don't want to discover, and I can't wait to spend my life unravelling the precious and mysterious riddle that is you, Ms Palumbo.'

The lump in Gina's throat clogged her airway as she submitted to Tara's kiss. She couldn't remember being happier. With this woman, surrounded by loved ones, everything seemed possible and wonderful. Except, Gina realised, it was her turn to speak. Tara squeezed her shoulder as she took the microphone.

'Um, okay, my turn,' she muttered, cringing as her words echoed through the speakers. 'I'm sure it won't surprise anyone to know I haven't prepared for this. I cannot emphasise how little I've prepared.' Her lips curled as the crowd giggled.

'I want to thank everyone for coming. It's a shame Tara's family couldn't make the trip from Perth. However, they've promised they'll be here for the wedding and are looking forward to meeting our friends. It remains to be seen whether they feel the same afterward.' She paused, grinning when a chorus of boos and whistles rose from said friends. 'To my colleagues, I really appreciate you being here, but if I could give you all some advice? It's okay to mingle with this crowd. There aren't any notable troublemakers.'

'Hey!' her friend Claudette yelled from the rear. 'What about me?'

Gina laughed, catching sight of the crown of bright blue hair bobbing above the gathering. 'Okay, so there's one notable troublemaker. But Claude aside, they're mostly civilised.'

She raised her arms across her face as cries of dissent arose from her friends. 'Sheesh, I take it back, okay? There are many uncivilised and rowdy characters. So, in conclusion, as you were, officers.' She finished by snapping off a brisk salute.

'Um, I have little to add except that Tara is my everything, my world, and I can't believe I get to spend my life with my best friend.'

She became distracted during their ensuing embrace by the sight of a uniformed constable, Anna Kopka, gesturing toward Munce. Her stomach dropped. Something had happened. Whatever it was, it was important enough for the young officer to crash her engagement party.

Gina frowned as she pulled away from Tara, her eyes locked on her superior's face as he conversed with the constable. His head snapped back, and he swung his gaze to meet hers before turning back to Anna. It may have been for an instant, but the expression she read there set her teeth on edge.

'Sorry, T. Give me a moment,' she said, keeping her focus on her colleagues.

As she neared, Munce raised a hand, but Gina jumped in before he could speak. 'I didn't expect to see you today,' she addressed Anna, who shrugged.

'Me neither,' the constable replied, her features pinched and smile fixed.

'What's going on, sir?' Gina turned to Munce. 'Is it another woman?'

'Let's not jump to conclusions, Detective,' he admonished. 'This may not be the same—'

'Yes, sir,' Gina interrupted, 'but . . .'

She trailed off when Munce raised a hand. 'Please, make my apologies,' he said in a low voice. 'I'll call from the scene.'

'I'm coming with you,' Gina announced. 'With respect, sir,' she continued when Munce opened his mouth, 'I'm coming.'

He appeared poised to argue but instead bobbed his head.

She pivoted to find her girlfriend standing with a group of friends. One look at Gina's face, and Tara shook her head. 'You're leaving,' she stated in a resigned voice.

Gina's skin flamed as guilt washed over her. It was their party she was leaving. Still, she had to see for herself if her suspicions were correct. She clasped her girlfriend's hands and leaned forward until their foreheads touched.

'I'm so sorry, T,' she whispered.

Tara drew away, a wry smile creasing her cheeks. 'I know, my love. Now go before I change my mind and chain you to a chair.'

Gina laughed as she turned to where Munce waited by the stairwell, Anna having left to wait in the car.

'Is everything okay?' he asked as she approached.

'Fine, sir,' she replied. 'She understands. Tara's not the problem. It's Dad. I've got an Anastasios special to look forward to once he realises I'm gone.' She grimaced as she imagined the ear bashing she'd soon receive.

George guffawed. 'We'd best make our getaway before he spots you. Otherwise, I'll be joining you in the doghouse.'

CHAPTER 3

ONCE SEATED IN THE passenger seat of the unmarked car, Gina spun to face Munce. 'Is it where the first bod—'
She stopped herself, having forgotten the promise she'd made herself after attending her first homicide. The vow to call victims by name came after observing the detached way many of her colleagues referred to casualties of crime. For them, it made the job easier to disengage from the sentient being with loved ones, dreams, and ambitions, now dead. Not so for her; she believed it made her a better cop if she made it personal. This came at a price, making compartmentalising difficult, blurring lines, and eating at her core. Her home with Tara had proved the only antidote, a sanctuary to stave off cynicism and hopelessness.

Gina's face blazed, and she stifled a groan. She should be with her fiancée at the party. The analytical part of her brain understood this, however logic wasn't the one behind the wheel right now. *Pun intended*, she thought wryly. The simple truth was, she had to be in this car, racing toward another crime scene. If it turned out her theory was right, she needed to see for herself.

She roused herself when Munce spoke. 'It's nearby, in the same vicinity.'

Gina swivelled to stare at the road ahead. She recognised his deliberate vagueness as a ploy to temper her belief that they had a serial killer operating in the city.

It was late afternoon when they pulled into a parking lot at the edge of the national park. Walking trails branched in three directions, disappearing into scrub, the smell of gum trees and eucalyptus assailing Gina's nostrils as she exited the car.

Before leaving home, she'd changed out of her party clothes into a pair of jeans and a long-sleeved top. When the breeze rushed through the cotton shirt, she reached back into the car to grab the jacket she'd thrown in as an afterthought.

Munce, having remained silent throughout the car trip, now took charge. He led Gina and Anna along the middle walking track, which was strewn with rocks and bracken, slowing their passage through the looming trees.

They'd been walking for ten minutes when voices filtered through the brush ahead. Munce led them around a curve where the trail straightened, widening into a glade the size of a racquetball court. Uniformed officers ringed the perimeter. They walked in a semicircle, their torches sweeping the ground. Police tape cordoned off the clearing where the forensics team now worked, their figures androgynous beneath their protective wear.

Detective Inspector Munce called to the nearest member, who approached them. 'What have you got?' he asked the bearded man, who glanced over his shoulder to where his colleagues huddled at the base of a gum tree.

'Sir, female, no identification. She's between the ages of 24 and 30. Long blonde hair, with an athletic build.'

'Cause of death?' Munce interjected in a sharp tone, causing Gina to glance toward him.

The technician froze before replying. 'Appears to be asphyxiation.' The man paused and cleared his throat. 'Sir, he bound her to the tree with rope and nailed her wrists to the trunk.'

Gina noted the colour drain from Anna's complexion. She patted the constable's shoulder before returning her focus to the techs moving like ants around the tree. With a quick glance skyward, she understood their haste. The light was fading fast as the sun began its descent.

'We need to look,' Gina said before checking herself. 'Sorry, sir.'

Munce brushed aside her apology and addressed the technician, who shifted on his feet, eager to get back to his work. 'We're coming in,' he stated. 'You stay put, Constable,' Munce ordered, and Gina's lips twitched when Anna sighed, her shoulders sagging.

'Detective, you're with me. We observe only,' he said as he held aside the police tape. 'Leave the evidence collection to these guys. I want you to consider the scene as a whole.'

Gina glanced at him, his turnabout complete now that he supported her theory. Her skin tingled, and her ears twitched as they approached the tree. Two of the technicians shifted to allow them a view of the body.

It was the same, Gina thought. The iron spikes, her torso falling forward across her bent knees. Jesus, she was right.

'It's the same killer,' Munce stated beside her.

Gina remained silent, eyes roving over the woman's body, blonde hair hiding her face. Was there something in the way he'd posed her, as if shielding her from their eyes? If so, why leave the bodies on a path used by locals and tourists, guaranteeing their discovery?

Then there were the iron nails. While investigating the first murder, they'd discovered they were old railway spikes, driven through Jenna's wrists with two strong blows.

The killer had suffocated his first victim with a soft object, a pillow or cushion. The coroner's office confirmed the presence of a powerful opiate in her bloodstream which, when administered in the correct dosage, rendered a person paralysed. It certainly explained why there were no signs of a struggle, no defensive wounds. The only marks were those left by chloroform around the woman's nose and mouth, suggesting the killer used it to disable her during the abduction.

Then there were the non-fatal injuries. Gina grimaced as she recalled the bruises and bite marks to Jenna's breasts and inner thighs. She shook her head to rid it of the images, noticing Munce talking with a senior technician. He caught her stare and held one finger in the air.

She retrieved the notepad she'd stuffed into the top pocket of her jacket, jotting down observations and details of the scene. Her pen twitched across the page as she described the visible injuries to Jane Doe's body. She stopped and stared at the corpse.

Sorrow infused Gina's chest, pressing against her lungs. Somewhere the young woman's parents fretted, not knowing what had happened to their daughter, fearing the worst. It may be a husband or boyfriend. *Or girlfriend*, Gina thought, shuddering as a picture of Tara's strawberry-blonde curls overlapped with the locks on the stranger nailed to the tree.

For a moment, her vision blurred, and her stomach flipped. Out of the corner of her eye, she saw Munce approach and inhaled, the air escaping in a whoosh.

'Have you got what you need?' Munce asked her.

'For now,' she replied. 'Did they find any identification?'

'Nothing. These guys will continue collecting and processing the evidence,' Munce said, gesturing toward the forensics team. 'Saunders will run the scene and coordinate a door-to-door canvas of the locals. I suggest you call it a day and go home to Tara. Get some rest. We've got a big day tomorrow.'

He waved her ahead and went to relay his final orders to the sergeant. Gina slumped under the tape and found Anna staring at her phone. While her complexion had returned to its natural rosy hue, pinched lips betrayed her anxiety.

Gina recalled her first crime scene: an old man, the victim of a random break and enter gone fatally awry. An iron pipe proved the murder weapon, multiple blows caving in his skull. She'd discovered then how difficult it was being part of the clean-up crew following the storm of human violence.

'We're leaving,' she announced now in a soft voice. Still, Anna started, juggling her phone.

On the ride back to the city, the young constable remained silent, her usual chatter forgotten. Gina used the time to arrange the crime scene in her mind. A killer's tableau – it was how he must have imagined it, she mused, a tremor rippling through her intestines.

When they pulled into the station's basement, Gina emerged from the car with a grunt. It seemed impossible only hours prior she'd been hosting her own engagement party.

'Shit!' she exclaimed with a furrowed brow.

'What is it?' Anna asked. She appeared ready to break, unable to take any more from this day.

'Nothing about the case,' she explained. 'I've just remembered I have an irate father and pissed off fiancée to face. It's not going to be pretty.'

She smiled when Anna laughed, pleased to find the constable recovered enough to find humour in her predicament.

When Gina reached her car, she scribbled the additional details she'd recalled during the car trip into her notepad. She even sketched the scene as best she could, given her limited artistic skills. Satisfied, she started the engine, grimacing when it sprang to life. She couldn't procrastinate any longer; it was time to face the music.

The drive to Bondi passed without incident. 'Typical,' she grumbled to herself; when she wished for red lights, they were all green.

Fifteen minutes after leaving the station, she slipped the key into her front door. The smile she'd rehearsed in the rear-vision mirror of her car faltered when she saw her father and sisters in the living room.

She swivelled to close the door, bracing herself against the weight of their stares. For a second, she paused, shutting her eyes and inhaling. Anna might not agree, but Gina preferred a hundred crime scenes such as todays to the Greek drama awaiting her.

CHAPTER 4

GINA GLANCED AT HER phone. It was after eleven, and her family had finally returned to their own homes. She picked up the empty mugs from the coffee table and placed them in the kitchen sink, weariness turning her movements sluggish.

As expected, her father and sisters had let her have it. They spoke over one another, their voices loud and words punctuated by agitated hand gestures. She'd gotten the gist – she couldn't expect her partner to put up with her disappearing acts, her work no excuse for abandoning their guests. It had been easier to appear contrite than to explain the demands of her job. Tara had remained silent during her family's tirade, disappearing after they left. Gina went in search of her now.

The sound of running water reached her as she approached the bedroom door. It surprised her to realise it was the bath, imagining Tara had gone straight to bed. Instead, she lay under a blanket of bubbles, one leg sprawled over the edge of the claw tub. Gina beamed, sighing when her girlfriend mirrored the gesture.

'I've been looking forward to this,' she announced, scooping a clump of bubbles which wobbled and glistened.

'Have you now?' Gina said, running her eyes over Tara's naked flesh. 'How was the rest of the party?' She perched on the porcelain edge and trailed her fingers through the suds, blowing them from the tips of her nails.

'It was fine,' Tara said. 'Everyone got wasted. It was a relief when they left. Animals.' She said the last with a breathy snort which made a conical imprint in the handful of bubbles near her face.

Gina watched her, heart swelling in her chest. God, how she loved this woman. She spotted a face washer on the vanity, which she grabbed and dunked in the water. It came up dripping, and she squeezed it before rubbing a cake of soap across it. She twisted until her back was to Tara, picking up her foot. She ran the washer across her toes, tracing the arch and heel before sweeping up her calves. Tara sighed, and Gina glanced over her shoulder to see her reclining with closed eyes.

'Gee, can we talk wedding plans for a moment?' her girlfriend asked.

'Hm,' Gina murmured, eyes tracing the line of her girlfriend's thighs. She leaned forward, running the face washer over Tara's knee and along the soft skin until it disappeared beneath the bubbles.

'I printed off a list of venues, and I . . .' She broke off with a guttural groan.

Gina raised the cloth, trailing it over the slight bulge of stomach poking through the blanket of bubbles. She loved how relaxed Tara was in her own body.

'You, Gina, are a thoroughbred race horse – muscular, strong, and perfect,' she'd announced early in their relationship. 'While I am one of those trail-ride nags with squat and rounded bodies, and a trail-ride nag cannot a racehorse be. So that's that.'

She loved Tara's paunch. It made her soft, curvaceous, and Gina wouldn't have her any other way. Now she traced the sloping flesh up her torso until her hand cupped the underside of a breast.

She abandoned the washer to twist and face Tara once more. Desire flooded her when she peered into beloved hazel eyes heavy with lust, her eyelids half-closed. She took a nipple between her thumb and forefinger, tugging until it hardened.

'Not fair,' Tara said, breathless. 'When I have time to talk to you, you go and . . . oh shit . . .'

Gina answered by sliding her hand beneath the water's surface once more, her fingers pressing into Tara until she flung her head back with a moan. She worked her thumb in a circular motion, moving two fingers back and forth until Tara's legs stiffened, a cry escaping her lips. She removed her hand and straightened her spine, suppressing a groan as it cracked into place. It had been worth it.

Gina didn't notice how much water had sloshed onto the floor until she tried to stand, slipping back onto her rump. 'That was close. I almost fell in,' she said, heart pounding.

'Gosh, how terrible!' Tara exclaimed. Before Gina could move, she grabbed her arm and pulled her into the tub. The latter spluttered as water sloshed over her, droplets stinging her eyes.

She giggled, strands of hair plastered to her cheeks. Swiping them aside, she rotated in the narrow space until she sat opposite Tara, knees to her chest. With one deft movement, she pulled her shirt off and threw it over the edge to land in the lake that had formed on the floor.

She leaned back, eyes fluttering when her earlier exhaustion overcame her. As her mind drifted, she brought her head upright to stare at Tara, who sat with her feet on either side of Gina's rump.

'What were you saying, T? Something about venues?'

Tara winced and wagged a finger. 'Not now, okay?' She bent her torso forward and reached a hand to stroke Gina's cheek. 'We need sleep, and it can wait.'

They left the bathroom in its state of chaos, throwing towels across the floor to soak up the runaway water. Gina shrugged out of her wet pants and underwear, leaving them among the debris. Naked, she followed Tara into their bedroom, falling across the bed without bothering to pull back the covers.

In a fog of exhaustion, she felt her body roll to one side and then the other, sighing when the duvet landed atop her. She thanked her girlfriend before darkness shrouded her thoughts and sleep claimed her.

CHAPTER 5

A FORTNIGHT HAD PASSED SINCE locals found the second victim. They'd identified her as Holly Fitzgerald, a 27-year-old executive assistant in a large city-based accountancy firm. Gina and Ravinder had interviewed her mother and grief-stricken father two days after they'd found the young woman.

'We didn't want her leaving home, let alone coming here,' Mrs Fitzgerald had railed. 'She wanted a change, she said. Got herself a job and left without a thought for her poor father and his health.'

Gina had glanced at the shrivelled man. He slumped against the seat cushion with his eyes downcast, and a picture formed in her mind. She'd recognised the dominant personality of the woman opposite, who could only express her anguish through indignant fury. No doubt the control she'd exerted over Holly sprang from a deep well of fear for her child.

As much as she'd sympathised with her, she understood the young woman's need to escape from beneath her mother's immense shadow. A lump had formed in her throat when she pictured the crime scene, Holly's quest for freedom having unwittingly led her into the path of a sadistic murderer.

Anger had welled as Gina had listened to the older woman speak, the paranoia she'd tried to pass on to her child. It made her more determined to find the one responsible for ripping this intrepid spirit from the world, her hopeful future stripped and nailed to a tree.

The press was across the story, especially after discovering Gina's involvement. After the events in the Blue Mountains, she'd gained a measure of unwanted notoriety. They'd quickly discovered Sylvia's identity as daughter of serial killer, Daryl Thompson, after which they'd resurrected the graphic details of his crimes and splashed them across all media platforms.

Gina hadn't been able to watch television or go online without seeing the same photo of the Thompson family that had hung above the mantle at Sylvia's cottage. Each time, she recalled when she'd first seen it, echoes of the shock and recognition that coursed through her at the time, taking the breath from her lungs.

Then the press had found Gina and the role she'd played in the story. Keyboard warriors dissected the case and her life, while workers across the nation gossiped around water coolers. The fact that she was gay and living with her long-time partner was the titillating cherry on top for reporters and punters alike.

For weeks after the Sylvia incident, journalists had hounded Gina at her new job as a probationary constable. They'd even parked outside her and Tara's Bondi apartment, waiting for either to emerge. Eventually, the news cycle had moved on, and they'd left Gina in peace. Now, five years later, they'd returned for their pound of flesh.

She had just shaken a reporter from the *Daily Telegraph* who'd waited outside the station to accost her as she went for lunch. 'No comment,' she'd replied to the young man's questions. It was a standard response she'd learned from her previous experience. Give them nothing, no words to twist to suit their own agenda and narrative.

'Are you okay?' Ravinder asked when she approached his desk. 'You look ready to bite off someone's head.'

'Not quite,' she replied, handing him a steaming coffee.

'What? You don't enjoy the fame?' he continued, eliciting a sigh from the detective. 'Many believe you love it.'

She glared at him, anger swelling in her chest. Her pulse thudded in her ears, and she exhaled, aware of her partner grinning at her. She sighed. 'I don't know why you're laughing, Ravi. You're the one partnered with the celebrity dyke.'

They both laughed, Ravinder's head bobbing in agreement. 'We outsiders have to stick together, yes.'

Gina nodded, patting his shoulder. She was the infamous gay officer who'd climbed the ladder using the step up she'd received – or so her naysayers believed. Ravinder was the turban-wearing Sikh who'd scrapped for every promotion with a quiet dignity his critics couldn't fathom. Together, they made an unlikely team that drew a range of reactions, from curiosity to distrust, through to outright hostility. Luckily, most of the animosity came from a shrinking breed of old-school cops. The rest came from a smattering of officers whose own insecurities fed their resentment, finding it easier to believe the pair's success was due to identity quotas and affirmative action, rather than personal achievement.

Gina acknowledged a dollop of luck in her fast track through the ranks. Her involvement in the Sylvia incident had certainly provided her a profile and reputation, while having Inspector Munce as her mentor hadn't harmed her chances either. What her critics refused to acknowledge was the hard work and long hours, the extra study that went into her advancement.

'Come on,' she said to her partner, who drank the last of his coffee, drying his lips on a paper napkin. 'Best we outsiders get to the briefing on time – if not early,' she added over her shoulder.

When they walked into the operations room, Gina caught Munce's eye, the inspector standing at the front of the room with two other senior officers. He dipped his head before returning his attention to the men beside him. She led her partner to two seats at the end of a middle row.

A few minutes later, Munce raised his hands until he had the room's attention. 'Right, there's work to do, so I'll keep this brief,' he began in a serious tone. It was his usual practice to begin these sessions with light banter. Not today. His mood swept across the officers, many sitting forward in their chairs.

For the next twenty minutes, he outlined the investigation, which was hampered by the lack of witnesses to the abductions and holes in the timeline of Holly Fitzgerald's movements the night she had disappeared.

When he stopped speaking, Gina watched his forehead crease, a shadow shifting across his hooded eyes. She understood his frustration with the lack of progress, answers, and suspects. To him, it was a personal failure.

'Neither crime was random,' he added. 'The killer is highly organised, planning his acts to the last detail, from the abductions to how he disposed of and displayed the women's remains. It's ritualistic, which makes him meticulous and hard to detect. He also left no DNA on his victims, traces of a common household disinfectant suggesting he wiped them clean before disposing of them.'

Munce glanced at the officers beside him. 'Gibson will concentrate on the Holly Fitzgerald murder and coordinate a blanket canvas of St Mary's station and surrounds. His team will meet after we break to get their assignments.

'Meanwhile, Simpson will continue to follow leads into Jenna Jacklin's murder, looking at everyone she encountered. Remember, he planned this. He learned her routine, and we need to do the same if we're to establish where he first saw her. We need to know why and how he picked these particular women.

'Right, that's it,' the inspector announced, shifting a folder in his hands. 'Remember, no detail is too small. If we do the work, we will find his mistake, and that's how we'll get him.'

The room filled with the sound of overlapping voices as the officers broke into groups according to their assignments. Except for a handful of detectives, including Gina and Ravinder, who looked toward Munce.

'You lot, with me,' he ordered, leading them into a small meeting room.

He spoke as soon as Detective Sergeant Cheng closed the door. 'While the others work on the individual murders, I want us to concentrate on the big picture.' He stopped and raised his hands, palms up in a welcoming gesture. 'So who's got any thoughts?'

'Sir,' Gina said, hiding her wince when Cheng glared at her, mouth open to speak.

He was one of those who resented her presence among their ranks, believing she hadn't earned it. A cynical man, his passion for the job had broken against the Cross. A notorious district of Sydney, Kings Cross was where the desperate, disenfranchised, and dalliers indulged in human frailty and vice. For officers such as Cheng, Gina's advancement was a kick in the guts. To add extra fuel to his burning resentment, she hadn't the baptism he'd had. Instead, to his mind, she'd slid from the streets of the North Shore into a coveted position in the heart of the action.

When Munce bowed his head, she brushed aside the detective's hostility and continued. 'I was thinking we should concentrate on the starting point of Jenna's trip.' She paused when she heard a snicker behind her. When she spoke again, her voice reverberated with annoyance. 'Sir, I believe Blacktown Station was important to the killer as an abduction site, but it's not where he found her, where he first encountered her.'

The room fell silent as the others contemplated her words.

'Why do you say that, Palumbo?' Munce asked, expression inscrutable.

Gina gulped and then shrugged. 'I can't say,' she began, her brow drawn into a straight line. 'It's a hunch, and I . . .' She trailed off as a few of her fellow officers groaned. She ground her teeth and thrust forward her jaw. 'It's as if he waits for the herd to thin.'

Munce interjected when a chortle broke the ensuing silence. 'That's enough,' he said in a stern voice, eyes zeroing in on the offending officers, whose grins dropped. He reset his focus on Gina. 'That's interesting, thinning the herd,' he said, head to one side. 'It might help the slow kids at the back of the class if you could explain what you mean.'

Gina glanced over her shoulder to see Cheng and his partner, Pritchard, redden and avert their eyes. She cleared her throat, mind scrabbling for the right words. 'Okay,' she began, a blush tingling the skin of her neck. 'Jenna worked at the offices of Santanos & Partners in George Street, catching the 5:35 p.m. train from Central Station every day. Except Thursdays, when she joined her colleagues at the Keg and Brew for drinks before taking the 8:53 p.m. train, arriving at Blacktown Station by 9:22 p.m.'

She sipped from the bottle of water she'd brought to the briefing. 'So here, you've got this hub of commuter traffic at Central, where a predator can blend in and lose himself in the crowds, his prey unaware of his presence. He spots her somewhere between the law offices and Central or at the station itself.'

Gina continued, her mind following the thread of her idea. 'But this allows for too many witnesses, so he follows to where she alights at Blacktown. Along the route, he becomes excited, his plans forming as each stop disperses more of the herd. Day after day, he rides the train with her until he finds the opportunity for which he's looking, Thursday-night drinks. He observes the carriages emptying, late-night commuters spilling onto platforms at each of the stations. She alights at Blacktown, one of only a few passengers. Now he has a time and place.'

She blinked, the scene of the young woman stalked by a faceless killer dissolving before her vision. 'So, he grabs her and, for hours, does whatever twisted, sick acts he wants. But when it comes time to dispose of her body, where does he take her? Even farther from the crowds. He takes her into the bush and leaves her.'

Gina spread her hands and shrugged. 'Prey separated from the herd. Her death comes far from the glare and lights. I believe his choice of dumping ground comes from more than simple self-preservation. It seems to me that he's making these women insignificant in death, plucking them from the spotlight and disposing of them in secluded shadow.'

She stopped and shook her head, eyes darting around the room, noting the glazed looks on her fellow officers' faces, as if entranced by her storytelling. That's what it was, a story. Still, it felt right, and she recognised the tingling sensation derived from intuition.

Meanwhile, Munce cleared his throat. 'Interesting,' he said, eyes delving into Gina's own. He nodded. 'It's a working theory,' he stated. 'Palumbo, I want you and Sular on the ground. Start by canvassing the station staff. Someone might have noticed something. Cheng, Pritchard, you start at Jenna Jacklin's place of work and go over the CCTV along the route to the station. McIntyre and Trelawney, you take the footage from Central.' He raised his hand when McIntyre opened his mouth to speak. 'I know we've been through them already. Look again. Keep your eyes out for anyone taking an interest in the young women coming and going.'

Munce stood upright, the others following suit. 'Okay, that's it for now. Report to me if you find something,' he ordered, eyes taking in each officer. 'Let's get cracking. We need answers, people. He will do it again. This, we know. We need to get a sense of this guy and how he's picking his victims if we've any chance of stopping him.'

Gina and Ravinder headed back to their desks in silence, each lost in their own thoughts. While her partner used the men's room, Gina pressed her forefinger against the image of Tara on her phone.

'Hi, baby,' she whispered a moment later when her girlfriend answered. 'How are you doing?'

She heard Tara sigh on the other end of the line. 'You're cancelling dinner, aren't you?' she said in a voice dripping with disappointment.

Gina winced. 'No,' she spoke, shame morphing into irritation. 'I'm not. I'll be there, I promise,' she added, holding her breath until Tara spoke again.

'Okay, great. Anastasios is bringing old photos of you he dug up,' she announced.

'Awesome,' Gina muttered. She supposed she should be thankful her father had waited this long to humiliate her.

They chatted for another minute before Ravinder reappeared, gesturing for her. When she joined him in the lift, she was grinning, the same smile she wore every time she spoke with Tara.

Ravinder looked at her from under raised eyebrows, which dropped as he smirked. 'You are so gay,' he said, head bobbing.

'Yes, Ravi,' Gina said with a laugh, 'I most certainly am.'

CHAPTER 6

'EUGENIA, YOU TELL TARA you don't want her working late,' Anastasios Palumbo ordered his youngest daughter.

'What's that, Papa?' Gina asked. She continued pouring wine for their guests, who filled the small lounge room. Not for the first time, she wondered whether she and Tara should upgrade to a larger place. It was fine before she had come out, when she'd kept the two parts of her life separate. While it was a relief to live an honest life, it became problematic when entertaining her father and two sisters, their husbands and six kids.

Not to mention Tara had expressed her desire to start planning their own family. Between the money from her practice and the pay increase that came with Gina making detective, they could afford bigger. In fact, if they juggled their finances, they could keep the Bondi unit as a source of income while buying a bigger apartment or town house.

'Eugenia, are you listening?' Her father interrupted her musings. 'Tara – she shouldn't be staying late at work. It's not safe.'

Gina glanced at her girlfriend, who grinned, eyes rolling. A smile flickered at the corners of her lips. It vanished under Anastasios's stern gaze. 'It's fine, Papa. Tara's a big girl, capable of making her own decisions.'

She balanced three wine glasses and delivered them, returning for the rest, a frown forming across her face. Loyalty dictated she stymie his interference even while agreeing with him. It had been a source of friction between them since Tara had first started the practice.

'There's no difference between your job and me seeing clients after hours. If I can accept and celebrate your career choices, then you should do the same,' Tara had stated.

It hadn't changed her mind when Gina pointed out her training and experience as a police officer. Nor the fact she had backup in the form of a partner while the psychologist had none. Instead of flogging a dead argument, she'd made Tara promise to schedule only long-standing clients and to keep the door to the building and her office locked.

When she rejoined her guests to find the conversation shifted, Gina sighed, shoulders dropping. Her relief proved short-lived when she realised they were discussing the investigation.

'Are you any closer to catching the monster who did this?' her sister Leda asked. Her eyes shone, the same grotesque and breathless curiosity reflected in the others' faces as they stared at her as one.

She perched on the arm of Tara's chair and straightened her spine, sighing. 'You know I can't discuss an active case,' she said, annoyance making her tone sharper than she'd intended.

'Oh, I realise that,' Leda breathed. 'But knowing there's a killer on the loose . . .' She broke off and shuddered, her husband Alesandro reaching to stroke her arm.

For crap's sake, Gina thought to herself. Now she'd have to soothe Leda's hysteria. She caught her eldest sister's gaze and stifled a giggle. When it came to their sibling's fragile nerves, Carin was her ally, the eye-roll one of hundreds they'd exchanged over the years.

She drew her expression into a neutral mask before addressing her sister's concerns. 'Leda, the chances of you encountering this man are remote, the odds of him targeting you even more so.'

A flush of annoyance rushed through her as she noted Leda's hurt expression, as if insulted by the suggestion she wasn't victim material.

Tara glanced between the sisters before suggesting a round of the Greek card game *kseri*, a suggestion greeted with cheers. She winked at Gina as she went to retrieve the deck of cards from their office. Love swelled in the latter's chest until she thought it might burst.

Later, in bed, Gina propped on one elbow, staring at Tara, whose lids fluttered and lips curled. 'The after-hour patients,' she began, reluctant to disturb her fiancée but determined to have her say now they were alone.

Tara's eyes popped open, expression defiant.

Gina brushed a strand of curl from her cheek. 'I worry for you,' she continued in a soft voice. 'There are plenty of creeps around, T.'

She stopped, images from the two crime scenes flashing before her. For a moment, she almost told Tara what was out there, targeting young professional women. Then she remembered their pact to keep work where it belonged, retaining their apartment as a haven, untainted by the ugliness of the outside world.

Meanwhile, Tara sighed. 'I get your job brings you face-to-face with the worst in humanity, and no doubt, that affects your view of people. But my clients are often those left in the aftermath. They are the damaged victims, for whom getting out of bed each morning requires all their courage. These people need access to services when they can make it, often outside normal office hours.' She paused and scowled. 'I can't do my job without inconveniencing myself sometimes, and I won't stop.'

Gina noted the way her chin thrust forward, the set of her mouth, and recognised she'd lost the battle, even before Tara sealed her victory with her next words.

'Besides, it's hypocritical of you. I live every day knowing your job places you in danger. It's difficult,' she stated, pain flashing across her features. 'But I cope because you're doing what you love and need to do. As am I.'

Gina ducked her head, thoughts jumbled. She wanted to tell her of the danger lurking in the shadows of society. Instead, she lay back on the pillow, folding her hands across her stomach. Tiredness spread to her extremities. As her breathing slowed, sleep tugged at her mind, lulling it into silence.

CHAPTER 7

OVER THREE WEEKS HAD passed since they'd found the second body in the national park, and Gina and Ravinder had returned to question their first victim's husband.

Troy Jacklin was four years older than his late wife. He had an athletic build, his features a pleasing symmetry; he was someone who looked after himself. *Not that you'd know now*, Gina thought when he opened his front door. Unruly stubble covered his chiselled jaw and cheekbones while dark bruising circled his eyes, which were a dull red.

Over steaming cups of coffee, Gina got to the point of their visit. 'Mr Jacklin,' she began after clearing her throat, pausing when he held up a hand.

'Please, Troy is fine.'

'Okay,' she continued. 'Troy, we've nothing new to report. Let us assure you, we're following every lead, canvassing areas around Blacktown Station and the route Jenna took home. We've got people doing the same at Central.'

She spread her hands in a helpless gesture. 'The man we're looking for is smart, thorough, and has at least a working knowledge of forensics. Enough to make our jobs more difficult, having left no DNA evidence at the crime scene or on either of the . . .' She flinched as distress collapsed Troy's face.

She sighed when Ravinder took over, his tone soothing and infused with calm authority. 'We are doing what we can, Troy, and I promise, we will catch the person responsible.'

Mr Jacklin gave Gina's partner a tremulous smile before sipping from a mug, which trembled in his hands.

'In the meantime,' Ravinder continued in the same tone, 'we need to ask you more questions. We'll be covering a lot of the same ground, but often it's the second or third time through when someone recalls a detail they overlooked or considered too small.'

Mr Jacklin nodded, his Adam's apple bobbing as he gulped back the tears squeezing from the corners of his eyes. 'Okay, I'm ready.'

Ravinder dipped his head to Gina, who opened her notebook and cleared her throat. 'Troy, you said Jenna mentioned nothing strange, no one watching or following her. Are there any details you've since remembered? An encounter which unsettled her, perhaps someone who paid her too much attention?'

She watched the man tip his head forward, eyes closed and brow furrowed. He remained in the same pose for a minute until he shook his head. 'No, nothing.' He opened his eyes and glanced between the officers. 'Everyone loved Jenna. She was a good person with a big heart.' His voice broke, and the detectives gave him time to compose himself.

'We need you to look at the crime-scene photos,' Gina said in a soft voice, reaching to clasp his hands. 'I know we're asking a lot of you,' she said, his panic palpable in his trembling extremities, 'but please, for Jenna.'

He drew in a trembling breath. 'I'll do it . . . for Jen,' he said in a firm voice, holding out his hand.

Ravinder passed him an A4-size print, which Troy took after a moment's hesitation. His breath sucked in as his eyes fell upon the image. In obscene detail, he absorbed the horrifying scene of his wife's death. It was a murderer's vision, and his expression reflected the shock and terror of Jenna's final moments.

His eyes narrowed, and his brow met between his eyes. He squinted, bringing the photo closer. 'Her clothes,' he muttered, his left eye twitching.

Gina leaned forward as he rotated the picture. She shook her head and glanced at him.

'They're not Jenna's,' Mr Jacklin exclaimed. 'I don't understand,' he said, his stare darting between the detectives.

'How do you know they're not your wife's?' Ravinder asked in an urgent voice.

'The dress. She owns . . . owned nothing like this,' he answered with certainty. 'Her clothes were more conservative, not so . . . so revealing.' His nose scrunched as he perused the clinging material that moulded his wife's body, cleavage visible below the hanging head, the hem riding her thighs so her underwear showed.

Gina glanced toward a bureau which held several photo frames. In each, Jenna's beaming face lit up the camera, her clothing fitted but modest. She recalled the dead woman's colleagues describing her as a professional in dress and behaviour. No, the clothing didn't match the woman she'd come to know during the investigation.

She peered at Ravi, whose eyes shone. This was an important clue, another detail to add to their portrait of the killer. Stripping his victims of their professional persona was important to him, needing to transform them into his image of women before meting out his punishment. She grimaced. It was easy to see how he viewed her gender.

Gina scowled, contemplating the predator they pursued. He would slip up, make a mistake. They always did. The question was whether they'd find it before he took another woman.

As if providence itself mocked her, the screen of her mobile lit up with a message. She glanced at it, heart skipping a beat. Too late – he'd taken and disposed of his next victim.

'What's wrong?' Troy asked, eyes anxious.

Gina peered at Ravinder, who bobbed his head. She reached to clasp the man's arm, giving it a squeeze. 'We have to leave, Troy,' she announced in a soft voice. 'We'll let you know of any progress in your wife's case.'

They excused themselves and left Mr Jacklin to his grief.

As Gina sat behind the wheel, eyes on the road, her mind drifted to the crime scene toward which they raced. Perhaps he'd made a mistake with this one. She gnashed her teeth together, wishing she could teleport them to the site instead of having to waste time in a car when the clue they needed to catch the murderer could be waiting for them.

They joined the M4, the freeway leading into the Blue Mountains, their vehicle weaving through traffic. When they passed the exit to the Northern Road, less than ten minutes from their destination, Ravinder's phone rang. He answered it with a stilted greeting.

Gina glanced sideways, heart tripping when she noted the colour draining from his face, the way his eyes widened and fixed straight ahead. A moment later, he ended the call with a final, 'Yes, sir. Will do, sir'.

Her eyes drilled into his profile. She returned her attention on the road in time to overtake a slow-moving vehicle. 'Well? What is it?'

Her partner shook his head, lips pressed together.

'Was that the inspector? What did he want?' She fired the questions at him one straight after the other, panic fluttering in her breast.

'We're almost there,' Ravinder announced as they began the climb at the base of the mountain. Gina concentrated on navigating the steep curve that dragged them from the flats that marked the western fringes of Sydney's sprawling suburbia.

The highway straightened and levelled as they headed into Glenbrook, the lowest town in the mountains. Gina slowed the car to take the first street, which wound past a row of shops before plummeting into a gorge skirting the edge of the national park.

They pulled into a small parking area crammed with police vehicles and two ambulances. It surprised her to find Inspector Munce waiting for them. She'd expected him to be at the dump site, overseeing forensics and the officers from major crimes. One look at his face, and Gina's heart stopped. With a thudding pulse, she alighted from the car, eyes fixed on her superior officer as he approached her.

'Gina,' he said, taking her arm.

His use of her first name scared her more, consternation tripping along her spine, her appendages trembling. 'What is it?' she asked in a quivering voice.

Munce muttered something she didn't catch, focused as she was on the sorrow infusing his tone and something else. *Anger*, Gina thought. He was furious.

'Who is it? Who's back there?' she implored, breath knocked from her lungs, the truth poking her consciousness. *No*, she cried silently. *It couldn't be . . .*

Oh Christ.

'No!' she exclaimed, her mind and body paralysed. 'No,' she repeated, the only thought she could articulate. Her head jerked, looking from one officer to the next. Their evasive and darting eyes sent an ache through her chest, bending her double. Nausea gripped her abdomen, squeezing and twisting until it erupted from her gaping mouth.

Convulsions tore her insides, the contents of her stomach spilling onto the dirt, splattering Munce's black shoes. Her brain froze, unable to compute what was happening. She sensed people moving by her with purpose but was alone with a razor-sharp anguish gnashing at her guts. She retreated to the single thought she understood – *no*.

Minutes passed as her legs shook, a freezing bolt of agony stabbing her calves and thighs. Strong arms held her upright, but she didn't recognise whose, only that without them, she'd have crumpled into a pool of her own vomit.

She heard a scream but didn't know from whence it came. *No!* This one syllable was where she now existed. If she lived. She groaned; this agony could only belong to life. It was Tara who didn't.

Then there was nothing.

CHAPTER 8

WHEN SHE CAME TO, Gina blinked in confusion. She was lying on a narrow bed, staring at a metal ceiling. A thermal blanket covered her, the silver foil rustling when she moved. She wriggled her toes, tilting her head when she noted their elevated position. A groan escaped her dry lips while a thumping began in her skull.

A voice cleaved her confusion. 'Gina,' it called, 'can you hear me?'

She blinked, surprised when droplets tumbled from the corners of her eyes. She lay on a stretcher in an ambulance. 'Was there an accident?' she croaked. Her mind scrambled to find her last memory.

Tara. The name flashed before her eyes. She snapped upright, her torso bursting forward in one motion, dislodging the blanket, which tumbled to the floor. For a moment, dizziness threatened to thwart her efforts. She inhaled a few shaky breaths and shook off the hands that grasped her arm to steady her.

'Get off me!' she cried, her voice coming in a hoarse roar. 'Get the fuck away from me.'

The man raised his hands and ducked his head. 'Okay, Detective. You're okay.'

Gina ignored the tone in his voice, the one used to placate a patient suffering a psychotic break. Was that what she was having? She swung her legs to the side until her feet touched the floor. When she rose, she swayed on trembling legs. She reached to grasp the nearest solid object, the stranger's outstretched arm.

'I'm fine,' she said, releasing him. 'I have to go,' she announced, moving in a crouch to the open door at the rear of the vehicle. Ravinder appeared from nowhere to offer his arm. She grasped it and lowered herself to the ground.

'Where is she?' The question entered the air between them as if spoken by a stranger.

The voice didn't resemble hers. It sounded faint, as if it had travelled a vast distance to reach her.

Her partner paused before tipping his head toward the walking track to the left. She moved toward the path on leaden legs, her feet working of their own accord, unfettered from her brain.

Branches brushed her face while she shuffled like someone blind. Ravinder appeared at her side, his arm linking through hers to guide her, steadying her when she stumbled over rocks and tree roots.

The glow from floodlights illuminated the trees ahead as the path widened. Gina hesitated, terror snarling at her mind. She whimpered, hand grasping her throat, squeezing until she gasped, her breath raspy. A figure emerged through the glare, taking a familiar shape as it drew nearer.

Munce stopped before her, eyes drilling into her as if trying to find the woman, the detective, he knew. She met his gaze and flinched.

'It's a mistake. It has to be,' Gina stated, head shaking. 'If he took her last night . . . Sir, this is a terrible mistake.' She broke off and pierced him with her stare.

He took her hand and squeezed before releasing it. When he spoke, his voice was that of an officer questioning a witness. 'When did you last see Tara?' If it wasn't for the way his voice had faltered on the name, she'd imagine him a stranger.

She opened her mouth to answer but then closed it again. A groan started in her gullet, rising with a hysteria that threatened to unhinge her.

It was after eleven when she'd arrived home the previous evening. She'd stayed late at the station to go over the case files, hoping to find a clue they'd missed. When she got back to the apartment, she'd sat on the couch with a cup of tea to try and unwind and forget work before joining Tara in bed. But she must have fallen asleep because when she awoke, it was to find herself scrunched against the couch arm, her neck at an unnatural angle.

When she'd entered the bedroom to find the bed empty with the covers in place, she'd assumed Tara had sneaked past her to get an early start at work. A common enough practice, it hadn't set off any alarm bells for Gina.

This wasn't happening, her mind raged, even while she registered Munce's clenched features. He was speaking again, but she pushed past him into the clearing.

Her nightmare blazed into colour, imprinting itself on her psyche. The forensics team at the base of a tall pine drew her attention, and her eyes zeroed in on the body fixed to it. Strawberry-blonde hair flashed beneath the floodlights, shimmering curls creating a halo. Familiar and beloved locks – she knew their silky softness, the scent of lavender-infused shampoo.

Convulsions gripped her stomach as she lurched forward, mouth gaping. With nothing left to regurgitate, yellow bile roared through her oesophagus with the intensity of a brush fire. Gina gripped her knees as she swayed on the spot. *Not now*, she ordered herself, sucking in the damp air.

A tremor began in her extremities, increasing in violence until her frame shook. Her teeth clashed together, jarring her jaw. She bit her tongue, mouth filling with blood. The injury barely registered as Gina teetered at the precipice. On the one side lay the soil, fallen leaves creating a blanket across the forest floor. This was the reality where Tara belonged – beloved, deceased Tara.

On the other side, a gaping chasm of black oblivion beckoned her, a place where her lover didn't exist nor the crippling agony and grief that accompanied her loss.

A blanket draped across her shoulders. She sensed its warmth but couldn't connect to it, the icy touch of shock paralysing her. She realised she was moving, leaving the clearing and its garish light. A part of her wanted to object, to insist she stay with Tara, but she didn't have the strength to resist.

Next Gina knew, she was perched at the rear of the ambulance, legs dangling into space. Nothing appeared real, not the emergency vehicle nor the officers who passed by her vision.

Someone handed her a cup of sweetened tea. When she took her first sip, Gina recalled the last time she'd experienced such a loss of time and autonomy.

It was after Sylvia had killed herself, plunging a needle full of snake venom into her neck. Her mind froze on the image of the older woman's body, a stiff plank suspended in mid-air as if she were part of a levitation act. Then came the bone-rattling tremor that had all but split her in half. The memory dragged Gina toward the darkness crouching in her peripheral vision, the precipice.

Caught at the juncture of shock and unspeakable grief, a commotion at the mouth of the bush path demanded her attention. She jerked her head to where four officers shuffled into the car park, a body bag between them. A cry wrenched from her throat at the sight of the zipper which ran its length. The officers glanced toward her before lowering their gazes.

She dropped to the ground and moved toward the second ambulance. Its doors stood ajar, two paramedics waiting to accept their cargo. That it was Tara, her Tara, was something Gina's mind refused to grasp. She stepped aside and watched numbly as the officers loaded the bag onto a stretcher that ran the length of the vehicle.

She was inside the ambulance before she realised she'd moved. Heart pounding, she crouched beside the bag, brutally black in its anonymity.

With trembling fingers, she grasped the zipper, holding her breath as the metal teeth opened in an obscene grin. Tara's unseeing eyes stared up at her, reflecting the finality of death. The soul which had shone through them had fled, leaving nothing but a shell of decaying organic matter.

Gina felt herself fall but was out before she hit the floor.

CHAPTER 9

G INA BLINKED AGAINST THE glaring lights. When her vision cleared, she glanced at the sterile white walls and overhead lights. The smell of disinfectant confirmed she was in a hospital room.

Voices broke through the fog, her father's among them. She sensed her sisters in the room, feeling the weight of their grief and dread.

'Argh,' she moaned, her throat raspy. She tried again, the attempt thwarted by a choking cough caught in her gullet. Her mouth opened as she gasped, tears stinging and veins throbbing. When her airway cleared, she pressed a hand to her chest, sucking in the precious air.

Her father barked an order, and someone placed a tumbler of water in his outstretched hand. He clasped Gina at the back of her neck, pulling her forward until she found the straw with her suckling lips. The icy liquid slid along her raw throat.

'Just a sip. Nurse's orders,' Anastasios whispered.

Gina lay against the pillow and waited until the room stopped spinning. When she was steady enough, she planted her hands on either side of her buttocks and propelled herself into a sitting position. The movement sapped her depleted strength.

'Where am I?' she croaked.

'Nepean Hospital,' her father replied. 'You are okay now, Eugenia. You are safe.' Tears slid across his cheeks, and she reached a hand to the side of his face where they fell. She stared at the droplets pooling before they traversed her knuckles and slid between her fingers.

'I'm okay, Papa. But Tar—' Gina stopped, unable to speak her name. A gut-wrenching wail tore the air, a noise cut off mid-note. She didn't recognise whose voice unleashed the unholy cry, only that it made the hair on her arms bristle and her scalp tingle.

'I'm so sorry, my child, my baby.' Anastasios spoke in a heavy tone. He dipped his head against the mattress beside her hip, sobs racking his torso.

'Where's George?' The question was the only thought binding her to reality. It also forced her father to gather himself, his sleeve mopping the last of his tears from his cheeks. When he next met her stare, she recognised the rock she needed. It was the strangest thing; while her organs continued their function to keep her alive, she felt completely eviscerated, an empty vessel.

Anastasios squared his shoulders and cleared his throat. 'Yes, George. He is on way. He come as soon as he heard you are awake. You rest now. He will be here soon.'

Her eyelids grew heavy, something resembling peace settling across her as her father stroked her hair. She had no idea how long she lay there before Munce's voice broke her inertia. With his usual authority, he ordered her family from the room before taking a seat on the edge of the mattress.

'Come,' he said, his arms opening to her.

Gina's eyes burned with tears, which she swallowed back, hands balled into fists at her side. She gasped as she fought the pangs, her mouth filling with blood as she bit her lip against the desolation threatening to erupt.

'Come,' Munce repeated, wiggling his fingers.

With a racking sob, Gina slumped forward. The world collapsed around her as she let go, waves of icy agony battering her innards. A strangled wail rose from the pit of her guts. She felt the inspector brace himself against the force of her anguish.

Gina abandoned herself to grief until the pain narrowed its focus, rage quelling the deluge. 'Sir,' she spoke, her voice low and ragged.

Munce held her arms and pulled away from her, finding her eyes with his. Whatever he read there reassured him as he stood and pulled a chair from the corner of the room. He placed it beside the bed and reached for the water on the table, handing it to her.

Gina imagined the motion of taking it from him before she did so, satisfaction washing over her when she executed the act. This small gesture of autonomy confirmed she could yet function, that her fury was the fuel she needed to endure.

Once she'd taken a few sips, she held the glass for Munce to take. 'Where's the investigation at, sir?'

Munce paused, his features drawing into a professional mask. 'He took her at her practice,' he said in a matter-of-fact tone as if it was just another case, one more victim. 'Officers found her bag on the corner of her desk, a patient file still open, and a pair of glasses beside her keyboard.'

'Was there . . . Did she fight?' Gina asked, cringing. She had to keep it together for Tara.

Munce shook his head. 'No sign of a struggle. Either she went with him by coercion or he disabled her before she could defend herself. We will need to wait for confirmation, however the same marks at the nostrils and lips as the previous victims would indicate the latter. scenario'

The relentless mechanisation of her mind whirred like an old movie camera, taking her to the scene of the abduction. Tara, her professional smile, greeting the faceless man before pivoting to enter the room she used for patients. The man, a fairy-tale monster, sneaking up behind her, his hand clutching a drug-soaked cloth. Perhaps she smelled it a microsecond before he grasped her, covering her face. Tara's body going limp in his waiting arms. The dark figure carrying her unconscious form to the vehicle he must have had waiting. He now wore a cape in Gina's mind, transformed into a Disney villain in her contrived scenario. She closed her eyes and willed her vision to clear, for the ghost of a hypothetical past to dissipate in a puff of mist. *For Tara.*

She inhaled a shaky breath. 'How did she die?'

Munce lowered his gaze, giving her the answer. Tara had been suffocated after the killer used the same narcotic he'd used on the others. Her mind fixed on a detail in the pathology report where it stated the opiate incapacitated the women while leaving their mental capacity unaffected. The thought of Tara conscious throughout her ordeal, aware of everything the man did to her without being able to stop it, brought a fresh surge of rage and anguish. It crashed against her chest, shaking her limbs.

'I need to get out of here,' she announced, scouring the room for her clothes.

Munce's hand on her arm stopped her frantic search. She stared at the hirsute wrist, blinking.

'Gina,' he whispered, 'they want to keep you overnight to monitor your blood pressure. You passed out twice, so you need to obey the professionals. If not them, then me. That's an order, Detective. You rest now.' Rising from his seat, he held up a hand to stop her from talking. 'I'll be back soon, and I promise to keep you updated. Now lie back. That's a good girl,' he said, tucking the end of the blanket under her chin, his gaze lowered before he turned to leave.

'One more thing,' Gina called from the bed. 'Has someone notified Tara's family?'

'They're on a plane now,' Munce answered before leaving with a last grim smile.

She realised she'd do anything to spare them the nightmare awaiting them after the long flight from Perth. That she could do nothing caused her airway to clog with frustration. The truth was she had no way of helping herself, and it rattled her to the core.

CHAPTER 10

G INA STARED AT HER reflection, zeroing in on the puffy skin framing her eyes. Her face appeared ghostly, cheeks sunken and complexion pallid. *Appropriate*, she thought, dragging at the bruised pouches, tracing the crimson web of veins criss-crossing the sclera.

She opened the vanity drawer, her movements lethargic as if she were doing everything underwater. The same as it had been every waking moment since Tara died nine days ago, each spent in a fog of grief. She grasped a make-up satchel and dabbed foundation under her eyes to cover the bluish-black flesh. Appearing less like a raccoon, Gina patted rouge to her cheeks to give them colour, before smearing gloss across her lips.

Tara's parents had landed the day after her body arrived at the coroner's office, where they identified their daughter's remains, holding each other as they howled their grief to unsympathetic walls.

Gina hadn't attended. Instead, she'd gone straight from the hospital to the station, hell-bent on seeing for herself how the investigation was progressing. She hadn't stayed long after Sergeant Anderson ordered her home when she'd forced her way into the evidence room. Crime-scene photos had blazed across her vision, wrenching a hoarse cry from her core, a wail that sent her fellow officers tripping over themselves to scurry from the room.

When she had followed moments later, she'd bolted from the station, trying to outrun the images of Tara pinned to a tree. But no matter her location, whether inside the walls that held them or at the Bondi apartment, she couldn't escape. She saw them every time she closed her eyes.

Tara's will contained instructions that her body be donated to science for dissection and study by first-year medical students at Sydney University. It was typical of the psychiatrist to help these burgeoning medics with their vital education, having been a strict adherent to the ethos of paying it forward.

While her parents understood and respected her wishes, Gina recognised the cost they paid not having a body over which to perform the rituals of grief and closure. It was why she'd agreed to hold a memorial service for Tara's family and friends, a chance to farewell her. While Gina had no intention of saying goodbye – she didn't know how – she hadn't the heart or will to refuse them.

Now the day had arrived, and she faced it with numb indifference. With a last sneer at the mirror, she walked into her and Tara's bedroom. 'Not anymore,' she muttered, the words dropping into the space, as lost and alone as she.

Silence fell across the apartment when she entered the crowded living room. Bec appeared from the kitchen and headed off the pack to reach her first, taking her elbow and steering her out the front door. With one foot in front of the other, Gina followed her along the hallway to the building's stairwell.

She'd stayed out of the arrangements for this day, but as she stepped onto the rooftop terrace under an overcast sky, she wished she'd objected to the location. Agony hit her like a punch to her abdomen, lurching her double.

With Bec's hand resting on her spine, rubbing in a circular motion, she straightened with a groan, eyes scrunched shut. She breathed shakily until the misery ebbed.

Carin appeared beside her, squeezing her arm and smiling through watery eyes. 'It's hard, impossible,' she stated, her gaze darting around the terrace.

Gina grimaced through trembling lips before sucking in another mouthful of air. She wasn't alone in recalling another day here, an occasion of hope and joy. It belonged now to another lifetime, and she suspected her life would be forever divided between her time with Tara and a post-Tara existence, however that looked.

Her sister led her to the front row of plastic chairs forming a semicircle. A fold-out table stood before them, draped in white cloth with photos of Tara adorning its surface. Gina screwed her eyes at the sight of her lover smiling and laughing, alive and vital. She slumped into her seat, lifting her buttocks to retrieve a folded programme placed there earlier by goodness-knows-who. Her mind shored itself against waves of despair crashing from every direction. Better the numbness.

The empty seats filled around her. Voices mouthed platitudes that meant nothing to her. Her father sat to her left, Barbara to her right, her sobbing a constant since she'd received news of her daughter's murder.

Anastasios spoke first. He expressed his love for Tara, breaking down when he mentioned her infectious grin. Gina's sister Leda rose and escorted him back to his chair, where he wept with head bent. Gina noted his pain in her peripheral vision but could do nothing for him. The underwater sensation hadn't abated, blurring her vision and muffling her other senses.

Tara's father, Tony, spoke next. He delivered a heart-wrenching eulogy through gulping grief. When he finished, he rushed to sit beside his wife, who moaned, her sobs melding with his own.

One after the other, those who'd loved Tara described her loving heart, her sense of fun and adventure. Their words hit Gina's eardrums, white noise unable to pierce her shield of enraged grief. If anyone expected her to speak, they let her be. How could she talk of Tara as if she was dead, gone?

The speeches over, friends removed the chairs, and the mourners broke into smaller groups. Gina watched the gathering from afar. People approached her but soon left when she didn't respond to them. She didn't blame them. They couldn't fathom she existed in a place beyond words.

Everyone except Munce, who stood at her left elbow, sipping his wine in silence. His presence was a concrete pillar upon which to lean, anchoring her to the world. It kept her from spiralling out of her body, pitching it over the edge of the building.

Gina started. The thought of plummeting to the street below, her skull exploding against the footpath, jolted her back to reality. She heard Tara's voice whisper in her ear, 'Eugenia, this is not you, my warrior princess. You are strong and fierce. This will not break you. You will survive this, love.' Gina could have sworn she felt a puff of breath against her nape.

Her eyes snapped open, and she gasped mouthfuls of air as if erupting from below the surface of a lake.

'Are you okay?' Munce's voice reached her, snapping her mind to attention.

'Yes,' she said in a strained voice, rough from disuse. 'At least, I will be,' she added with a grimace. With a shaking hand, she squeezed his arm and walked toward the nearest group of friends. They welcomed her with exclamations made louder by the fact they were on their third or fourth drink.

Tara's words replayed in her head as she tried to follow the conversations happening around her. She was right, Gina thought, as usual. She'd survive, live on without her best friend and lover, and she had just the tool to help her. With fury to fuel her, her mind filled with one idea: revenge.

The fact that she survived the next few hours, she attributed solely to alcohol. By the time the crowd thinned until it was only family and a handful of close friends remaining, a buzzing filled Gina's head.

'You're not leaving?' she slurred when Bec and Akeisha approached her.

'We have to get going,' Akeisha announced with crinkled brow. 'But we wanted to tell you something before we leave . . . in private.'

Gina glanced between them, confusion swimming in her booze-addled brain. She grabbed an unopened bottle of champagne and led her friends to a cluster of chairs at the farthest corner of the rooftop terrace. Slumping into the closest one, she popped the cork, bubbly spilling over her arm.

'Gee,' Bec said, 'we want you to come and stay next door. It's empty, and we think it would be good for you to get out of this place. At least for a while.'

Gina tipped the bottle to her lips, the liquid missing her mouth and splashing onto her shirt. 'What next door?' she asked, mopping the silk fabric with her sleeve. 'You're not making sense.'

Her friends exchanged a glance before Akeisha grasped her hands. 'Sylvia's old cottage. You remember we bought it?'

'Kay,' Gina mumbled, a memory breaking the surface of her drunkenness. She recalled her friends breaking the news to her and Tara. It was years ago now, and in her current state of mind, it wasn't surprising she'd forgotten. Now the conversation came rushing back to her.

'What?' she'd sputtered. 'How the hell did that happen?'

'Sylvia's will,' Bec had stated. 'She included provisions giving her tenants the option to purchase their property with her estate acting as mortgagors. It was an incredible opportunity, and after discussing it, we decided we'd be idiots not to take it. I mean, how often do you get the chance to enter the property market without having to come up with an exorbitant deposit? Then our circumstances changed, and we discussed with Mr Langley, the estate lawyer, about the possibility of also purchasing Sylvia's place to use as a holiday let for extra revenue. He agreed, and so . . .'

'But . . . but how were you able?' Gina had asked, her expression incredulous.

Akeisha had blinked back tears. 'Nana – it seems she was savvier with her finances than we'd realised.'

'The woman was a tycoon,' Bec had added with a chortle.

Gina had met Akeisha's grandmother years ago, not long after they'd become friends. She'd been anxious meeting a woman from her generation. Even though she'd accepted Keish and, by extension, Rebecca, it didn't necessarily mean she was open to all their lesbian friends.

Her fears had proven unfounded when the grey-haired woman beamed, grasping Gina's hands and enfolding them warmly in hers. 'I'm so pleased to meet you, dear,' she'd said. 'I've heard so much about you. I feel as if I already know you.'

Later that same evening, she'd told Gina something that had stayed with the young woman. It came after she had asked the older woman how she'd reacted when Akeisha told her she was gay. She'd glanced around the sitting room filled with religious icons scattered among the furnishings and adorning the walls. This was before she had come out to her family, so there was more than simple curiosity behind her question.

'Ha,' Akeisha's nana had replied, cherry-coloured cheeks splitting into a grin. 'I already knew, of course. She was never interested in boys.'

Gina had pondered this, building up the nerve to ask her next question, one she wouldn't normally ask of a near-stranger. 'But what about him?' She'd dipped her head toward a copy of *The Last Supper* suspended above the doorway into the kitchen.

'Honey,' the woman had replied, patting Gina's arm, 'my God doesn't make mistakes. Anyone with two eyes and half a brain could see our Akeisha was born this way, as natural and beautiful as any of his creatures. Besides, I love my granddaughter, and I couldn't be friends with person, or deity, who'd condemn her to hell, including God. Forgive me, Father' – she'd crossed herself – 'but it's the truth.'

Gina's mind had retreated from that first meeting to find Akeisha still talking.

'After we sold her place in Balmain as well as two residential properties and a commercial building in Glebe she owned, we were able to buy not only our house but also next door.'

'We're going to use it as a holiday rental,' Bec had added.

Gina recalled the first trip she and Tara had made after their friends had purchased the property. She'd been torn between happiness for them and dread at visiting Sylvia's old cottage.

The memory faded, and Gina thudded back to the present, her head fuzzy and spinning.

'I loved your nana, Keish,' she slurred, hand groping for her friend's arm. 'She was nice.'

Gina noticed the couple talking but couldn't focus on their words. A minute later, someone dragged her to her feet, which stumbled as they led her toward the exit stairs.

'Sorry,' she grunted, head hanging forward, with her chin resting on her chest.

The last she recalled was flopping onto the bed she and Tara had shared, someone leaning in to whisper in her ear. 'Shhh, you sleep now.'

CHAPTER 11

G INA WINCED, HER SHOULDER burning where she'd slammed it against the door frame. Vodka sloshed above the rim of her glass, splashing onto the carpet. She stared as beads of liquid soaked into the fibres, spreading and imprinting the pile. With a shake of her head, she focused on the couch four or five paces from where she swayed.

She pushed herself off the wall, reeling from side to side as she zigzagged across the room, flopping onto the couch cushions, dislodging another wave of liquid.

Gina couldn't recall how much time had passed since the memorial service. She remembered a phone call from the local gym wanting to speak to Tara about renewing her membership. After that, everything became a blur.

She groaned, head dropping into her hands. An image flashed before her vision of a large man with a leathery face and a mouth of yellowed teeth. A name nudged her consciousness, drifting from her muddied thoughts: Shorty.

At once, a faint scent drifted into her nostrils. It was a mixture of body odour, urine, and stale cigarettes. The smell jolted a memory from her clouded mind. It evoked a picture of herself squatting on her haunches, surrounded by a group of vagrants and rough sleepers who called the arches and tunnels of Central Station home.

A bitter sneer twitched Gina's lips as she recalled the bottle of cheap booze this version of herself had clasped. At least, the week-long stakeout had allowed her to indulge in her new relationship with alcoholism, she thought, her stomach growling.

She hadn't been out of place with her dishevelled clothes, hair unwashed and oily, and breath a rancid mix of cheap booze and unbrushed teeth. It was on the fourth day when she'd met the large man of indiscernible age.

During this period, she'd gained a degree of understanding into the dispossessed souls who inhabited the streets. There'd been moments when her skin flushed with shame as she recalled the dehumanising language some of her colleagues used when discussing the homeless of Sydney. Her blush had deepened when she replayed her own homogeneous response, a tepid defence of the vulnerable hadn't known nor cared to.

It explained the innate distrust with which these people viewed her profession. The way many faded into the shadowy nooks of buildings whenever a cop came into view was nothing short of impressive. She'd shrunk with them on the second day when two members of her team, DCs Edwards and Tyson, had appeared, presumably to ask questions about the dead women.

They'd walked past the enclave in which she cowered without glancing her way, and she'd thought then how the department was ignoring a valuable resource in these people due to a long history of mistreatment and harassment.

When she'd met her new friend after many days and sips from the vodka bottle she clutched to her chest, she began the same speech she'd recited half a dozen times without getting a single bite. Until now.

'Saw this real creepy guy a coupla days ago,' she said in a low voice, eyes scanning the motley group for a reaction. 'He was following this lady. Looked like he was up to no good.'

'Unsnipped prick,' someone guffawed. For a second, Gina couldn't tell from where the voice came. She leaned forward to peer around a huge man to where the speaker dissolved into a fit of laughter.

The broad face of the man next to Gina split into a wide grin. 'He means uncircumcised, miss,' he said in a gravelly voice. 'The hooded pecker, we call him. On account he always wears the same hoodie and looks like a dick. Hasn't been 'round the last few days. But he'll be back. No good, that one.'

It had been another two days before the man they'd named the hooded pecker returned, and during that time, Gina got to know the man with the ironic nickname Shorty. Gina learned the one who'd spoken, a younger man named Trevor, had latched onto the man-mountain two years ago, soon after he ran away from home.

'Someone has to look after Trev,' Shorty explained with a shrug when she questioned their relationship. 'He's a good lad. Not his fault his father was a vicious drunk.'

As for the gentle giant himself, he told Gina he'd arrived home after losing his security job over a year ago to find the locks changed and his belongings scattered across the front lawn.

'She's poisoned my three girls against me,' he said, referring to his ex-wife with a flash of bitterness. Next second, his shoulders slumped. 'Don't blame her or the girls. I was drinkin' heaps, gambling too. Not much to be proud of here.' He gestured to his figure, cloaked in worn and dirty clothes, a blanket dotted with holes draping his torso.

Gina had patted his wrinkled hand, sorrow swelling in her chest.

That was when Shorty leaned forward and whispered, 'The hooded pecker.'

Gina had followed the direction he pointed to, where a male wearing faded jeans and a dark hoodie skulked near the entrance to the station. His hands burrowed into his front pockets while his head slumped forward. Gina sensed rather than saw his eyes darting, searching.

She'd observed him for over an hour before he made a move. When a young woman dressed in a skirt and blazer hurried through the entrance, the man followed her into a tunnel which ran the length of the station, ramps leading up to the platforms.

Gina only just made the westbound train, joining the throng of commuters squeezing through the packed carriages in search of seating.

She'd stood in the entranceway, where she was able to duck her head to spy on the man who sat behind his prey in the downstairs compartment.

When the train lurched, she'd grasped one of the steel poles to steady herself but not before stumbling against the knees of a businessman who glared at her in disgust. Gina had forgotten she still wore the guise of a vagrant, including the ripe odour clinging to her clothes. She ignored the man in the suit and bent her head for another glimpse of her quarry. He was gone. She could still see the woman, but her stalker had disappeared.

While the train clattered along its rails, she'd crept down one step and then another until she spotted the man's denim-clad legs. She descended one more step until more of him came into view. He was holding something in his hand. It was a camera pointed at his intended victim, sitting diagonal to him now. She retreated to her position by the pole, much to the disdain of her new pinstriped friend.

Stop after stop, commuters pushed past Gina, but they'd been of no interest to her. Finally, at St Mary's Station, the young woman mounted the steps beside her, standing close enough for Gina to touch. She was in her late twenties, her long auburn hair streaked with blonde highlights. Her body was fit and curvy beneath a tailored jacket she wore over a pleated skirt. When Gina had squinted, the woman's image superimposed over those of the dead women, including Tara.

She'd watched after her with an aching heart as she alighted onto the platform. After she'd disappeared, Gina focused on the single file of passengers as they filtered past her. No Hooded Pecker. She'd dipped her head and placed one foot on the lower step when his figure sprang up in front of her vision. For a moment, their eyes had met before she stepped back to allow him passage. She'd counted to three before she bounded after him, spotting his hooded figure standing at the bottom of a set of stairs, staring at the commuters climbing them. When Gina crept closer, she saw the young woman disappear at the top.

The man had remained where he was, his hand reaching for something from his top pocket. A flip-style notepad flashed as he drew out a pen and scribbled across the page. When he'd changed platforms and boarded a city-bound train, Gina blended in with the crowd behind him.

When they'd reached Central, Gina trailed him through the throngs, keeping her distance as he shot out the far side and approached a white van parked in an alley at the back of the station. She'd waited behind a concrete pillar. Two minutes passed before the vehicle drove by where she stood, the words on its side clear as day. It was a courier van.

For three days, Gina returned to the same spot where Shorty, Trevor, and their group spent most of their days. Each day, the hooded pecker kept his vigil, waiting for the same woman, following her onto the train bound for St Mary's. She was his next intended victim. Once Gina was certain of this, she'd bidden her new friends farewell.

'Good luck, Tara,' Shorty said with a raised eyebrow.

Gina wasn't sure why, but it was the name that had slipped out when she'd first introduced herself. She paused and took one of his huge paws in her clasped hands. 'I'm not . . . that is . . .' She trailed off when he snorted.

'You're a cop,' he stated, sending Trevor into fits of laughter. Shorty had grinned when her eyes widened. 'Knew straight off but figured you had your reasons for hiding it. Was obvious you didn't want your mates to see you neither, considerin' you hid behind me every time one came along.'

Gina had sighed, her head dipping. 'I am, only I'm not exactly officially working . . .' she began before wincing. Could she be any more cryptic?

Apparently, it was enough as Shorty nodded. 'As I said, good luck to you. I believe your intentions are . . . not good, perhaps, but just.'

Gina had hugged the giant and then Trevor, who giggled and squirmed from her grasp.

Now back at her house, many days and drinks later, Gina roused herself. With a grunt, she scanned the coffee table for a space to put her glass. She blinked and drew the surface into focus, the rest of the room spinning and tilting, the tumbler slipping from her hand. It landed on the carpet, standing on its edge before toppling over, its contents rushing out in a wave.

She bent her head to stare at the spreading stain, her heaving stomach making her snap upright, the motion sending the room into a whirl of colours and shapes. The couch cushion rushed at her, striking her cheek and jarring her jaw. Gina heard a loud groan before her mind pitched into darkness.

CHAPTER 12

A BITTER ODOUR WAFTED INTO Gina's nostrils, which scrunched in protest. The drum pounding against her temple intensified as she lifted her head. One eye opened a slit, grit clinging to her lashes. When her vision cleared, she recognised the Norman Lindsay nude framed on the wall above the television. She was home, in her living room. A tentative smile tugged at the corner of her mouth before despair rushed through her chest, clawing her heart and lungs.

These were the best and cruellest seconds of her day. In this minuscule window of time, everything was okay. It was a precious space where Tara lived still, just offstage, waiting for her cue to enter. *Except she never would.* Gina couldn't stop the thought from expanding until it blotted everything else until there was only the smothering blackness of a reality in which her lover didn't exist.

Through stinging tears, she fumbled along the glass-top table until her fingers brushed the corner of a bag. It was Ziploc plastic inside which lay a neatly-folded blue sweater. Gina positioned her nose above one end before sliding the latch open, her nostrils flaring as she breathed in Tara's scent. She pressed the bag against her chest.

As much as she longed to hold the jumper in her hands, to rub its softness against her cheek, she didn't want to waste what perfume remained. She coveted it, only allowing herself three deep breaths before closing the bag. Gina understood it was a finite thing, this rush of love and closeness to Tara, and dreaded the moment the scent faded to nothing. She instinctively understood it would be akin to losing her all over again.

Now a different smell assaulted her, the stench of something rotten. Her stomach flipped, and she clasped her hands over her mouth. She gulped and lowered her eyes until her tracksuit pants came into focus. Dried chunks of half-digested food covered her crotch – and something else.

Shock stilled her addled thoughts as tears burned behind her eyes. She blinked, salty droplets splashing onto her stained sweatshirt. The damp cloth of her pants clinging to her buttocks and thighs brought a wave of red-hot shame. Urine mixed with vomit to create a ripe stench which assaulted her senses.

At the corner of her vision, a bottle came into focus, half its contents still intact, sunlight piercing its liquid and making it gleam. With trembling fingers, she clasped it and raised it to her trembling lips, where it mingled with her tears. The first mouthful of liquid fire shot through her gullet.

'Fuck,' Gina slurred, tilting the bottle again, warmth spreading into her chest and extremities, bringing with it a tingling numbness.

'Fuck!' she cried. It was a bellow that came from nowhere, from everywhere. She lurched to her feet, dislodging lumps of vomit from her lap. They landed haphazardly, blending with the spilled vodka to create a Pollack style pattern.

Bent forward, Gina planted her palms on the edge of the coffee table. She used it to support herself as she navigated its corners, straightening when she reached the other side. The door to the bathroom swayed in front of her, and as she pitched forward, her feet tangled and sent her sprawling to where the carpet met the tiles, her chin cracking against the porcelain.

Pain exploded through her head, her teeth clashing and rattling, blood filling her mouth. She shifted her head, resting her cheek against the cool surface. Her jaw throbbed, so she opened her lips and moved it from side to side, sighing. It was intact, so there was no need to visit the hospital. She couldn't stand it, anyone seeing her now. Her grief was her own. It was ugly, messy, and it stank, but it belonged to her.

Even as this thought filled her mind, she sensed prodding from her subconscious. An idea she'd set adrift on a raging sea of alcohol now clamoured for her attention. Her head still resting on the porcelain surface, Gina sensed a shift within her. It flashed before her, a single truth. This was her rock bottom, and covered in her own sick and piss, she wallowed in its wanton depths.

There was something comforting in the idea, and she let it wrap around her. She felt safe in the simplicity of the choice before her. Either she embraced the bottom, losing herself in a pit of despair and degradation, or she moved and, with the only direction being up, returned to life.

'Tara,' she moaned, the image of her lover floating before her vision, eyes twinkling as if Gina's terror-induced paralysis was a big joke.

The grin spread across ghostly features. 'Get up,' lips whispered without making a sound.

'I will,' Gina said. 'I will, T. I promise.'

She pushed her torso off the ground, legs straining to bring her upright. With a final sway, she shook her head and marched through the doorway into the shower receptacle. Without removing her clothes, she turned the knobs, icy water eliciting a stream of profanities.

By the time the hot water kicked in, the globules of vomit were making their journey through the drain grate. With heavy movements, her fingers clasped at the waistband of her pants, dragging them across her hips until she shimmied them off her legs. Her underwear and shirt followed, until she was naked, arms at her side with palms open as the deluge washed away the last vestiges of her drunkenness.

After several minutes, she wrapped herself in a clean towel. Gina was herself again. Edges still frayed and veins holding more vodka than blood but still more herself than she'd been in weeks. Beyond the inevitable hangover, she welcomed the wave of fury crashing against her innards as an old and dear friend. She needed its support, the crutch it provided imperative for her to carry out her plan. No longer could she wade in self-pity, despair coaxing her into catatonic inertia.

While she'd tried to drown her thoughts in a deluge of boozy forgetfulness, her brain cells had rallied, crafting a road map for revenge. The first part: to get rid of all remaining alcohol, her flirtation with the bottle at an end. She needed a functioning brain to thrash out the final details of her plot. For Tara, she had to move forward, rejoin reality.

After all, the being she sought belonged to the living, the one who owed a blood debt for her lover's death.

CHAPTER 13

THE NEXT WEEK, GINA sat outside Munce's office. She shifted in her seat, glancing at the time on her phone. He was late, which was unlike the inspector. She rifled through her bag for gum, head snapping back when his voice reached her.

'After my meeting,' he spoke to somebody out of sight. Next second, he rounded the corner from the lifts, smiling when he spotted her. 'Detective Palumbo, good to see you,' he said, grasping her hands when she gained her feet.

'Thank you, sir,' Gina replied, following him into the office.

Once they were seated, Munce assessed her, eyes lingering on her sunken orbs with their black rings. 'You haven't been sleeping,' he observed, to which Gina shrugged. He appeared to want to say more but instead reclined in his chair, fingers forming a steeple below his chin. 'So, what can I do for you?'

Gina cleared her throat. 'What's the latest? Any suspects or leads?'

Munce considered her while she fidgeted beneath his scrutiny.

'Sorry I dropped off the radar,' she muttered, dropping her gaze. 'I couldn't handle . . .' She broke off, eyes darting. 'I needed time alone.'

Munce dropped his hands to cover hers. 'You don't owe me an apology, Gina.'

The detective's eyes pooled, and she shook her head. 'For Tara,' she whispered, repeating her new mantra until her tears abated. When she met the senior sergeant's gaze, they were dry.

Munce withdrew his grasp. 'Hmph,' he grunted. 'As for progress, we have no suspects, although there are a few persons of interest we're investigating.' He raised a hand when she opened her mouth. 'I can't give you names, as you know.'

Frustration clogged Gina's airway, and she sucked in her breath, exhaling the air in a high-pitched whistle. With a curt nod, she gestured for the inspector to continue.

'We're following up on the clothes the victims wore,' he continued, his features a mask of professional blankness.

Gina winced. In this building, Tara was a victim. Her importance lay in the fact that her name made a murderer's kill list.

As if reading her mind, Munce's eyes softened. 'I know it's Tara,' he whispered. 'She's more than a victim. We will get the person responsible. That's a promise. Everyone in this station wants to get him, for you and for Tara.'

Gina's lips twitched, head bobbing.

He cleared his throat and opened a file. 'Clothes are different brands, most available through the big retail chains: Target, Myers, et cetera.' He looked up from the paper. 'There is something I need to ask – did Tara wear nail polish?'

The question jolted Gina, and she shook her head. 'No,' she replied before pausing and tilting her head. 'I mean, sometimes for special occasions, but they weren't painted when she . . . disappeared.' She gulped. *For Tara*, she mouthed, cringing under Munce's gaze. 'Why? Were they painted?' she queried in a high-pitched tone.

Munce examined her before he nodded and drew a photograph from a file on his desk. Gina recoiled, eyes flashing and heart hammering. The inspector waited with the image facing the desk. When she squared her shoulders and met his gaze, he flipped it over, the picture bursting into garish colour.

The photo showed a pair of hands – Tara's hands. Gina noted how clean they looked. She perversely wished they were filthy – bloody, even – a sign of how hard she'd fought her killer. But she knew her girlfriend hadn't the chance to fight back, courtesy of the drug in her bloodstream. The fingernails flashed blood red, filed and buffed to a high sheen.

'No,' Gina exclaimed, tapping the edge of the print. 'She never used this colour. I'm 100 per cent sure, sir.'

Munce replaced the photo in the file. 'I suspected as much. So, he's bathing, dressing them, and doing their nails.'

Gina started. 'Oh my god,' she whispered, colour draining from her complexion. There was something intimate in the killer's grooming ritual, as if he cared for these women. *Before he snuffed out their lives,* she thought, fury chasing off nausea and despair.

'He cares for them,' she repeated aloud. 'The time and patience he takes to go through the same routine . . . Sir, he loves them. At least, he loves his image of them.'

Munce dipped his head. 'Agreed. I believe we're dealing with a different killer, someone who forges a romantic attachment to his victims. But not before he transforms them from professional women – elusive, out of reach – into the type of female he sees as accessible, ripe for the picking.'

'He needs privacy and time,' Gina chimed in, 'which suggests he's single, living in a free-standing house, not an apartment or similar. Hard to move bodies in and out of a shared building without anyone noticing.' She stopped, glancing at Munce, who grinned.

'It's good to have you back, Detective,' he said.

Gina jolted. 'That's it, sir. I'm not. Not back,' she mumbled, tiredness seeping through her pores.

Munce's grin dropped. 'That's fine, Detective.'

Tears prickled Gina's eyes. She needed to wrap this up, impending exhaustion and grief threatening her control. 'Sir, I don't know how long I'll need. I can't . . . I can't come back to work. It's too much. I'm barely able to . . .' A sob welled through her gullet, and she gulped, forcing its retreat.

Meanwhile, Munce grasped her hands again. 'I can arrange for a month's special leave. If you need more, we can discuss options then. How's that sound?'

She nodded without speaking, a lump wedged in her throat.

'Do you need to collect anything from your desk before you go?' Munce asked in a tight voice.

K.J. STEWART

'I'm right,' she replied. 'I grabbed what I needed before coming to see you,' she added, averting her eyes.

'Gina, is there something you haven't told me?' he asked with a raised eyebrow.

She glanced at him before answering, 'No, sir, I don't think so.' His stare bored into her profile until she forced herself to face him, shoulders slumping when he nodded.

There was no way for him to know so soon what she'd done. It would be at least another day or two before anyone realised she'd run the plates from the hooded pecker's van through the system. It was not a matter of *if* but *when* they discovered her transgression, and Gina knew she was living on borrowed time. The best she could hope for was a couple of days' head start, her plan hinging on it. Regardless of the consequences to herself and her career, it had been worth it. She had a name.

'If you need anything, anything at all, please let me know,' Munce said, his eyes gentle and full of concern.

She let his words wash through her with a mixture of triumph and guilt. The first part of her plan achieved, Gina excused herself after promising to take care and to keep in touch. Her thoughts chafed and raw, she hurried through the back corridors and out via the underground car park to avoid having to speak to her partner or colleagues.

She needed to get home and pack. The next stage of her plan awaited, and now she had the killer's identity, she didn't have a moment to lose.

CHAPTER 14

'JESUS, I FORGOT HOW freezing it gets here,' Gina exclaimed, rubbing her hands in front of the fireplace.

'It is winter,' Akeisha retorted and then blushed. 'You're right. It's freezing,' she added, glancing at Bec, who shook her head.

'It's good to see you, Gee,' the latter spoke, eyes drilling into her. 'We've been worried for you.'

Gina hid her sigh. 'I know, and I'm sorry. It's . . . it's still difficult to face people. Everyone wants to help, but no one can. They just need to leave me alone.' She broke off and spread her hands. 'That's why I'm here. It's the ideal spot to retreat and hide from the world, to lick my wounds, and I can't thank you guys enough for letting me stay.' She tilted her head in the direction of next door. Gina still couldn't think of the cottage as belonging to Bec and Keisha. To her, the setting was as much a part of Sylvia as her arms and legs.

The couple exchanged a glance before Bec addressed Gina. 'We understand and promise we won't intrude. Don't we, Keish?' she added pointedly, dipping her head when her girlfriend nodded.

'Take whatever time you need,' Akeisha gushed. 'But we're here for you, okay?'

Gina smiled. 'Thanks, Keish, but if you don't mind, I might head next door and get settled,' she said, holding her breath until her friends offered to help unload her things from the car. She refused, promising to call later when she'd unpacked.

Her shoulders sagged when she navigated the neighbouring driveway. She turned off the engine and stared at the cottage. For minutes, she sat, studying the facade. It looked the same as when she'd first approached it, and the hairs on her arm bristled when she recalled how anxious she'd been.

With leaden limbs, she climbed the steps to the front porch, much as she had five years earlier. Back then, her imagination had gotten the better of her, and it seemed nothing had changed. For a moment, Gina had to fight the compulsion to retreat, to get into her car and drive off the mountain. But where would she go? She wouldn't – or couldn't – go home. There was no such thing without Tara.

No, she'd choose a direction and keep driving until the land ran out, an inevitable outcome when you lived on an island continent; sooner or later, you had to reach a shoreline. Even as she pictured it, the wind in her hair and the open road, she sighed and slid the key into the lock, pushing against the door.

It opened with a creaking noise, and her heart skipped a beat. Despite the cottage's former owner being long dead, in the faded afternoon light, it was easy to believe her spirit lingered. Memories of Sylvia greeting her that first morning played before Gina's vision, her mind conjuring the image of the old woman with silver hair in a bun.

She closed her eyes, and when she opened them, the hallway was empty. Reaching around the door frame, her fingers fumbled for the switch. A second later, the foyer burst into light. She cast a furtive glance toward the sitting room, where she'd sat with Sylvia, before hurrying past it to the kitchen.

Her heart lifted at the sight of a vase of purple hydrangeas on the island bench, together with a basket of fresh fruit. When she investigated further, she saw her friends had stacked the fridge and cupboards with food for her stay.

There was a binder on the marble countertop, and Gina opened its cover. It was information for visitors in relation to the cottage's amenities as well as local attractions and eateries.

Next to this sat a guestbook, and she sat at a stool and thumbed through its pages.

"Thanks for the perfect week. The cottage is well appointed while maintaining its old-world charm. We enjoyed the fireplace in the sitting room and spent many happy hours in front of it. Thank you – we're already planning our next visit."

"What a gorgeous cottage in a beautiful setting! After a day of bushwalking, shopping, or sightseeing, it was the perfect place to unwind in front of the fire with a glass of wine. Thank you for providing a home away from home."

Gina closed the cover after promising herself she'd read more of the entries later – if she got the chance.

When she carried her cases through to the guest bedroom, she noted there was fresh linen on the bed and the window was opened a crack to air out the musty space. She admired the care and detail her friends had put into the place to make their guests feel welcome.

Her movements robotic, Gina unpacked her case, hanging clothes inside the wardrobe while folding the rest into a timber tallboy. When everything was packed away, she drew a binder from her backpack. She brushed a hand across its cover before striding through to the lounge room.

She placed the folder on the coffee table and stared out the floor-to-ceiling windows to the garden. The light was failing, and she couldn't make out the third level of garden where the land plummeted into a gorge with deadly abruptness. With a shake of her head, she swivelled and lowered herself to the couch, opening the file.

Following her stake-out at Central, she'd rung the courier company whose logo ran the length of the hooded pecker's van. After two attempts, she'd spoken with the manager, who had confirmed the logo was out of print. As to the specific vehicle, it was ex-fleet, the company having upgraded six months ago. It appeared the young man wasn't working as a courier but instead using the ruse to move around unnoticed.

Then had come her professional misdemeanour, accessing the force's database for personal reasons. Despite her niggling shame, she still couldn't regret it. She had his name: Benjamin Foster, the man who took Tara, murdering her for his own sick needs. The address on his licence was in South Penrith, at the base of the mountains. According to her enquiries, five tenants lived in the rental property, four of whom were unemployed, including her suspect.

His living situation bothered her, convinced as she was that the perpetrator needed privacy and space. Still, everything else pointed to Benjamin's guilt. *He must take them to an unknown location*, she mused, fingering the copy of his licence.

Not for the first time, she debated calling Munce to use the department's resources to take down the murderer. But as before, she dismissed the notion. She was too far into her plan now. For Tara.

Tiredness seeped through her limbs, and she closed the file and pushed it across the coffee table out of reach. Her stomach growled, and she pondered making herself a sandwich. The idea swam in murkiness, the swirling tentacles of sleep choking it, dragging it into the darkness where hunger didn't exist.

CHAPTER 15

PANIC RUSHED AT HER when Gina's eyes snapped open to seamless darkness. Her pulse raced, and her breath came in panting gasps. Where was she? Bits and pieces of the past month penetrated her mind, and she clung to the facts she understood. Tara was dead. She, Gina, was staying at Sylvia's cottage in Leura, and she had a plan. Her heartbeat slowed and breathing eased.

She'd fallen asleep on the couch, her body creaking when she sat upright. After stretching her muscles, Gina bent forward in her seat, reaching her fingers to tap across the surface of the coffee table until they stumbled across her phone.

With the illumination from its face, she rose and shook her legs, blood tingling through her feet and toes. Her eyes blinked until they focused on the time: 4:37 a.m. Too early to be up, too late to sleep. Gina showered, standing with bent head beneath the cascading water. Her finger moved across the glass screen, crafting Tara's name in the steam. She watched as the letters distorted before trickling down the pane in rivulets.

By the time she had dressed, brushed her hair, and cleansed her face, it was 5:30 a.m. and still pitch-black. She made herself toast, mentally thanking Akeisha and Bec when her teeth sank into the homemade raspberry jam. With a steaming cup of coffee beside her, Gina returned to the file on Benjamin Foster. She flipped open the cover of her notebook, pen twitching across its pages as she made notes, a macabre to-do list. *Soon, there would be no retreating.* The thought triggered a ripple of nausea she gulped back, driving it down with another scorching mouthful of caffeine.

Half an hour later, an orange glow lit the horizon, and Gina relaxed against the couch cushion and watched it grow brighter, shrugging aside the dark cloak of night.

As soon as the garden emerged through the gloom, she roused herself, grabbed her phone, and strode onto the rear deck. Her eyes darted to where, five years earlier, she'd seen the animal cage with the shed skin of its deadly prisoner. A shiver rushed across the skin of her arms, hair bristling. She focused forward and shook her head.

There was no time for distractions. It had to be today. If she didn't do it now, Gina was worried the voice in her head, Tara's voice, would sway her from her course. Either that or Munce would discover her plan and put a stop to it. Neither scenario was acceptable. In this new world of heartache and agony, she couldn't live with this man breathing, going about his depraved existence, while her lover's corpse lay in a refrigerated drawer.

Frost turned the lawn a sparkling white, and her feet made a crunching sound as she crossed the top stretch of lawn. She stopped and glanced behind her at the perfectly formed imprints left by her shoes, her breath coming in puffs of steam. Stomping to keep warm, Gina continued to the next tier.

When she reached the stairs leading to the lowest level, she ordered herself to focus, pressing the face of her phone until she set the timer. After retreating to give herself a run-up, Gina took a breath and pushed through the balls of her feet. Four strides, and she leaped from the edge of the stairs, arms swinging and torso bent. She landed and, in one fluid motion, sprang forward. After four strides at pace, she slowed, the seventh step bringing her to a halt a metre from the gorge's edge.

She bent double, hands on her knees, sucking in mouthfuls of frigid air which burned her oesophagus. It took a minute for her heart to stop pounding. After repeating the same exercise several times, Gina returned to the cottage and jotted figures into her notepad.

To keep busy and rein in her fevered thoughts, she began exploring the cottage. At first, it had surprised her to find it largely untouched, just as Sylvia had left it. As she walked through its walls now, she recognised the appeal of the old-world experience the mountain cottage provided its guests and acknowledged it was a smart business decision to retain its ambience.

The only difference Gina noted was the renovated bathroom, where a vanity and shower receptacle sparkled white in their newness. They'd kept the claw-tub set near a window with a view to the garden, and in under any other circumstances, she'd be enjoying a soak and a glass of wine.

Gina headed to the former owner's room, where she rifled through an antique timber wardrobe. A garment bag hung in the farthest corner, and when she examined it closer, she saw it contained two woollen coats and the white dress Sylvia was wearing when she'd first encountered her. Her mind conjured up that first meeting, the old lady ageless as she danced and twirled at the base of the apple tree. She wondered if Bec and Keish had kept these items for her.

Gina asked herself what Sylvia would make of her intentions, the path she'd started mapping after Tara's murder. Somehow, she felt the old lady would approve. In fact, she may be the only person who'd have understood.

After she finished her scuffling, she moved onto the room at the far end of the hallway. It had belonged to the friend, Freya, who'd shared her life with Sylvia before losing it to cancer. She stood at the window overlooking the garden, barren branches tapping against the glass panes. The image of its occupant looking out at the same view floated behind her closed eyes. A swelling bubbled in her chest as she recalled the story Sylvia had recounted of Freya's abusive childhood.

The furniture in this room was French Provençal, a white dressing table beneath the corner window drawing Gina's attention. She pulled open the top drawer, straining when it caught on its sliders. It was empty. She was pushing it closed when she noticed something odd. The depth of its interior didn't align with its frame.

She opened its twin and frowned. The first was shallow by half in comparison, and she peered closer and swept her palms across its timber bottom. It felt less solid than its counterpart to her touch.

She pressed against it, her frown deepening when it buckled in the middle. With a probing touch, Gina's fingers ran over its edges until they met a corner which depressed when she exerted pressure. When she withdrew her hand, it lifted, revealing a small gap. She drew in her breath.

Her pulse racing, she hooked a nail under the raised lip until there was a tiny popping sound. It was a false bottom, a panel inserted and fitted to conceal a space between it and the drawer's frame. She lifted it free and placed it atop the dresser.

A diary filled half the space, a wooden box the other. She picked up the latter and lifted its lid. A ballerina popped upright, its figure dressed in a ruffled tutu, her feet en pointe. It rotated as the soft strains of classical music drifted through the air, caressing Gina's ears. She'd heard it before but couldn't recall the name.

With careful movements, she slid it onto the dresser top and reached a hand toward the diary. Fingertips a centimetre from its cover, she hesitated. Dread crept across her skin, leaving her flesh vibrating. She shuddered, a shadow shifting across her thoughts.

'Get over yourself,' she whispered, drawing it from its hiding place where it had sat, presumably, since its author's death. She rubbed a hand across the hard surface, dust particles dancing through the beams of light penetrating the window. For a minute, she didn't move, the journal heavy in her hand.

A small padlock sealed its contents, and Gina peered into the drawer in search of its key. It wasn't there. She searched the other drawers but came up empty. With a grim expression, she strode from the room and made her way to the kitchen, where she retrieved a knife from the cutlery holder.

She screwed her eyes and slipped the narrow blade between the curved metal that looped through a top hinge. By increments, she applied more and more force until it snapped, the padlock skittering across the floor tiles. She ignored it as she stared at the pages that burst open to reveal a neat scrawl made in a fine black point.

A name jumped out at her, and she snapped the diary shut with a sharp intake of breath: Sylvia. She didn't feel strong enough to cope with any fresh revelations regarding the woman who'd come to hold an almost mystical place in Gina's memories.

With deep breaths, she stared at the cover with its rose print. *Who are you kidding?* she chided herself. She had to look if for no other reason than her curiosity overpowered her dread. With a flash, she recalled the saying about the fate of cats who succumbed to this emotion. *Well, this feline is willing to accept the risk,* she thought with steely resolve.

She glanced about until she located the mug of coffee she'd abandoned before her search. With a grimace, she noted the scum settled across its surface and thrust it into the microwave. When it beeped, she clasped it, warmth spreading through her palm.

Gina was grateful for its heat when she stepped through the doors to the back deck and the icy air embraced her. She ducked her neck into the hood of her jacket before plonking herself onto a cane chair set near the edge of the deck. With a deep sigh, she gulped a mouthful from her mug before opening the journal at the first page. She began to read.

> Every night I return to the basement. I see the staircase leading into the subterranean rooms below my family home. The nightdress the girl wore reached her feet, and it opened and closed when she navigated the barely lit steps. I watch her from outside, an observer to her terror, a silent witness to her pain.
>
> This disconnect ends when she steps into the light. At once, I am catapulted inside her flesh. I peer at the faceless men through her eyes, cigar smoke distorting their features. Their breath, a mixture of tobacco and whiskey, assaults my nostrils as they pant above me, their penises penetrating the girl's privates. Their hair-covered paunches flap against her flat stomach and chest, stealing the breath from her lungs.
>
> Every night, over and over, I return to the basement until I don't believe it will ever end. I fear I'm bound to revisit the scene of my torture and degradation for the rest of my days, which I will welcome with open arms.

K.J. STEWART

Droplets splashed across Gina's cheeks, tumbling onto the page. She blinked and tilted the journal on its side until the beads of liquid ran off, blurring the inked words of the bottom line. With pursed lips, she blew against the paper until the ink dried. It was still legible.

Thank goodness, she thought, placing the diary on the glass table beside her. She stared at the words she'd read, stomach clenching against a stirring nausea. Jesus Christ, she wasn't ready to read this – not now. Still, the words flew off the page, lodging themselves in her brain.

Gina shook herself and gulped. She couldn't afford to lose herself in Freya's horrific life, her misery. She had too much of her own. Not to mention if she wanted the plan to succeed, she needed complete focus.

After several minutes, she felt fortified enough to return the journal to its hiding spot in Freya's old room. There would be time to examine its tale later. For now, she had shit to do, and after a quick glance at the time, she shoved its existence into the far recesses of her mind and sprang into action.

CHAPTER 16

GINA WENT STRAIGHT FOR the gym bag sitting on the kitchen table, the sound its zipper made reminding her of the body bag in which they'd carried Tara's corpse out of bushland. Anguish clawed at her heart and lungs. She waited for it to pass, leaving her raw, wounds jagged and bleeding.

With a grunt, she finished checking the bag's contents. She fingered the glass vial of chloroform, tipping it with her thumb against the stopper. Two rolls of tape, handcuffs, and a rag completed the kit. It occurred to her she was indulging in a ritual which mirrored that of a serial killer, a thought she hastily shoved to the darkest nook of her mind.

At lunch, she forced a sandwich past the nerves bubbling in her throat, waiting half an hour to make sure she wouldn't regurgitate it. With a last glance in the hallway mirror, she pinched her cheeks before dragging a woollen coat over her sweatshirt and jeans. She extinguished the fire she'd lit in the sitting room that morning, casting her eyes about to make sure she had everything in place for her return. With a nod, she opened the front door and stepped onto the porch.

She pulled a pair of mittens over her fingers and breathed hot air into them, stepping off the front veranda. After the short walk to her friends' house, her cheeks and the tips of her ears stung.

The door swung open to show Bec restraining her girlfriend with an outstretched arm, one Akeisha pushed aside as she rushed to hug her. 'It's great having you here,' she gushed. 'Next door, but still . . .'

Bec took her arm in a gentle grasp and tugged her away from Gina, who laughed.

'Thanks, Keish,' she said, shocked by the sound. She grinned at her friends, content in the simple enjoyment of their company. They beckoned her in, Akeisha taking her coat while Bec led her into the lounge.

'Keish, honey, have you finished packing?' Bec called over her shoulder, pivoting to face Gina, who stopped before the fire grate. 'Remember, we're only going for one night,' she added with a wink.

A giggle erupted from Gina's mouth, her hand racing to stifle the noise. She squeezed her eyes as tears welled, blinking when a hand rested on her forearm.

'It's okay for you to laugh,' Bec whispered. 'It's not a betrayal.'

She rubbed Gina's hand, comfort spreading from her at the unassuming contact, which demanded nothing from her. It was the most intimacy she'd shared in weeks, and she gave Bec's hand a pat before stepping back to put space between them.

The ensuing awkwardness dissipated when Akeisha joined them, a suitcase stuffed to the brim in her hand. Gina glanced to find Bec staring at her. The two women chortled, while Akeisha frowned and pouted before joining their laughter.

'Here's the key,' Bec said after they recovered.

'If you need anything or you get spooked, come here,' Akeisha said, ignoring the eye-roll from her girlfriend.

'Shit, Keish,' Bec said with a grin, 'she will not get spooked. Not our Gee.' She slung an arm across her shoulders. 'Not fucking Wonder Woman.' She squeezed until Gina grunted.

'I'll be fine, Keish,' the latter said, rubbing her arm. 'It is only a night.'

'We'll be home after lunch tomorrow,' Bec confirmed while Akeisha hugged Gina, blowing a kiss over her shoulder as she walked outside where her girlfriend's four-wheel drive sat.

Gina stood on the porch and waved as it disappeared around the bend in the driveway. She sighed, clasping her hands together. With the front door closed, she leaned against it, heart tripping inside her chest.

She shook herself, rushing back to Sylvia's cottage to change clothes. She grabbed the gym bag and her notepad, hesitating at the front door. Who was she, and of what was she capable? *Whatever it took*, she decided, her chin thrust forward, *for Tara*.

With hurried movements, she locked Sylvia's place and retraced her steps next door. With a final breath, she walked into the foyer and snatched a set of keys from a hook attached to the wall. The metal sat against her palm, and she stared at it, heart thumping.

Outside, she watched the lights on Akeisha's SUV flash as the door locks released. Gina grabbed the roll of narrow black tape from her bag and cut strips from it. On her haunches, she strategically placed the pieces across the front and rear plates, altering the letters. When she stepped back to observe her handiwork, she nodded. It wouldn't hold against scrutiny, but from a distance, it would pass.

Gina threw her bag across the back seat and swung herself into the driver's seat. She stared at her reflection in the rear-vision mirror. What she was planning was a criminal offence, a gigantic leap across the line. Now was the time to stop, to abandon her mission, and to err on the side of sanity.

'No,' she snapped, the image of Tara nailed to a tree filling her vision. She shook her head and swiped at her face with an open palm until the picture disappeared. When the engine roared to life, Gina frowned, faithful fury hardening her resolve. *Let's do this*, she ordered herself, slipping the car into first gear.

CHAPTER 17

THE FINAL BLAZE OF sunlight came in hues of orange and red. It resembled a blazing fire behind the weatherboard house, providing it a somewhat regal visage, its shabbiness muted in the glow.

She'd pulled Akeisha's SUV against the curb of the house in South Penrith. The inhabitants of the property Gina watched were home. *All except one*, she mused. She was banking on the others being too wasted or distracted by the boring monotony of their lives to notice her lurking presence.

She'd spent the earlier part of the evening parked behind Benjamin Foster's fake courier van. It was a risk, waiting there when she had no way of knowing this wasn't the night he would snatch his prey. Different scenarios took the air from her lungs, all ending with another woman's death while she sat twiddling her thumbs.

That it would be her fault weighed against her chest. She'd found their killer and had knowingly and with criminal complicity kept it from Munce and her colleagues.

When he'd come into view, she'd exhaled a hissing breath, her stomach lurching. Her mind on autopilot, she'd trailed him onto the freeway leading west, overtaking him to give herself a head start to his address. She'd prayed beneath her breath that he was going home and not lying in wait for his next victim.

Now doubts once again plagued her as she drummed her fingers against the steering wheel, nerve endings tingling. The idea of driving back up the mountain and forgetting this madness flooded her mind. She could call Munce, give him Benjamin Foster wrapped in a bow, and let the chips fall where they may in terms of her career. To this point, the only crime she'd committed was a misdemeanour, and she doubted she'd even receive a citation given the circumstances and her unhinged mental state. The killer would be their problem, and they'd use their considerable resources to apprehend and prosecute him. He'd be convicted to life behind bars, and she'd be off the hook.

Perhaps it was time to process Tara's loss and resume her career, her life, whatever that looked like. The problem was when she tried to imagine it, she came up blank.

While she pondered a Tara-less existence, she heard the sound of an approaching vehicle. The window closed on thoughts of retreat, and peace settled across her mind, as if the decision was out of her hands. At least, she wouldn't be responsible for another woman's death this night.

Gina peered at the set of lights in the rear-vision mirror. She squinted against the glare as she swivelled to catch the name of the courier company as the van passed. She waited while it pulled into the driveway. Eyes focused ahead, she unstopped the vial from her bag, tipping its pungent liquid onto a rag. She opened the vehicle door and slipped into the dusk.

With the cloth stuffed into her jacket pocket, Gina flattened her skirt at the knee. With trembling fingers, she checked to make sure her bun was still intact. She wasn't the best hairdresser, but she'd practised using a YouTube video and believed she passed as a professional – with a hint of nasty. Gina hoped this combination, together with the easy pickings she offered, tempted him to overlook the fact she didn't match his type. At least enough to pique his interest, which was all she needed.

The breath she inhaled shook, so she took another to steady herself. *It's now or never*, she told herself, the man out of the van and approaching the house on foot.

'Excuse me,' Gina called, arm raised. When he swivelled to face her, she simpered, a hand fluttering to her throat, a jittery, vulnerable bird. 'My car broke down, and I was about to start door-knocking for help.' She paused and dropped her fingers to where her cleavage showed. 'But no need now you're here.'

Gina dropped her eyes before meeting his beneath fluttering eyelids. 'I've no idea what's wrong, and my phone is dead. I'm stuck.' She watched him hesitate, his eyes shifting toward the house. Her breath stopped. He wasn't going for it. Then he smirked, his cheeks creasing in the gesture. *Jesus, he was young.*

With a shrug, he dropped his bag and stepped toward her with a sneer, not sensing a threat from the stranded young woman.

'Thanks so much,' Gina gushed, eyes wide and blinking. 'Tools are in here.' She motioned to the rear door, shifting to allow him access.

He winked when he stood beside her, and Gina hid her flinch, instead flashing him a coquettish grin. As he bent forward, she removed the rag from her pocket, reaching around to clasp it over his mouth and nose.

Her arms clamped around his writhing torso, she used her weight to restrain the man's arms as he pushed against her. She clung to him, breath coming in pants, until his body went limp. With a small cry, she released her hold, his body flopping across the bench seat. Her head turning to each side, she scanned for witnesses. When everything remained as it was, she shoved the man farther into the car, tucking his legs behind the driver's seat.

Back behind the wheel, she tilted the mirror until she could see his sleeping face. Her heart thumped. She'd done it. *Not the time to celebrate*, she chastised herself, shaking her head. She accelerated along the street, leaving the house and empty van in the SUV's mirrors.

Careful to stick to the speed limit, Gina guided the car through the back streets of Penrith until she took the ramp onto the freeway at the foot of the mountains. Time passed in a silent bubble as she carried her unconscious cargo up the winding road. Her eyes darted between the road ahead and his serene face. He looked like a child in repose. Panic gripped Gina's stomach. What if she was wrong? He didn't look like a cold-blooded killer.

Halfway to her destination, nausea gripped her stomach, and she pulled into a rest stop, flinging open the door. Her hands clasped her mouth as she stumbled to the bushes at the side of the road, fingers spreading to allow vomit to splash and drip to the ground. When it stopped, she wiped her hands across the leaves of a bush, grateful for the dense branches hiding her from the view of passing motorists.

Back at the car, Gina opened the rear passenger door and leaned forward until her face hovered inches above Benjamin's. She noted his eyelids flutter. With a grunt, she reached over the seat to grab the gym bag from the passenger seat. She doused the rag with more chloroform, clasping it over the man's face. Satisfied he wouldn't wake for the remainder of the trip, she resumed her position and directed the SUV back onto the highway.

Twenty minutes later, she pulled into Sylvia's driveway. There'd been no noise or movement from the rear seat, so she rushed to open the front door before returning to drag the man from the car. His body slumped to the ground. After taking a deep breath, she bent forward and clasped under his arms. With laborious steps, she dragged him across the gravel and up the stairs to the porch.

Gina rested him against the front of the house while she straightened her spine, moaning when it seized, and a spasm shot through her lower vertebra. She shook her arms and once again bent forward to grab her load. Bottom first, she heaved her load into the house, the man's body clunking across the raised threshold. With gritted teeth, she strained and grunted as she manoeuvred him into the sitting room off the front hallway, the room where she'd listened to Sylvia's life story.

With a last effort, she pulled the limp body to the chair she'd placed before the wood burner, groaning as she hoisted him into a sitting position. She stood upright and stared at him, hands on her hips, head to the side. Exhaustion threatened to overcome her, so Gina forced herself to keep moving. She went out and retrieved her gym bag, which she brought inside and placed on the table beside him.

The handcuffs clinked as she drew them forth, moving to the back of the seat. She wrenched the man's hands together. When the cuffs locked into place, she rattled them before scuffling through the bag once more. The thick tape screeched as she tore a length of it and fixed it across the man's mouth. She then wound it around his ankles over and over until she'd secured them to the chair legs.

He wasn't going anywhere when he awoke. If he did. Gina reached a hand forward and placed the back of it under his nose, stilling herself until she detected a faint puff of breath. He was alive – for now.

With a last glance, she left the cottage one more time to return Akeisha's car to her friends' carport. She crouched at the front and then the rear, removing the strips of tape from its number plates. Last, she entered the house on silent feet and returned the key to its hook before retreating and locking the door behind her.

For a moment, she stood, breathing in the frosty night air. It was six thirty, but the light was long gone from the mountain sky. Her breath shook as she inhaled, listening to the beat of her heart slow. She'd done it. She had him. It was his time to bleed and beg for mercy. But not before she got answers.

You won't get them standing here, she admonished herself, cupping her bare hands and blowing hot breath into fingers frozen blue. Rubbing them together, she hurried back to Sylvia's cottage.

Gina paused with her hand hovering above the front-door knob. Inside were the answers as to why her life lay in tatters, her lover ripped from her. She sucked in a lungful of air and squared her shoulders before striding through the doorway and into the sitting room. She was ready for him, Benjamin Foster.

CHAPTER 18

'WHA . . . Where am I? What's happening? Who the fuck are you?' The questions fired from the man even while Gina ripped the tape from his mouth.

She watched him try to focus. His eyes rolled back in their sockets, pupils dilated, and she leaned in until her face hovered above his. 'Is that what they asked, Benjamin?' Gina emphasised his name.

'How . . . how do you know...?'

His unfinished question hung in the air between them, and she met his gaze, lips pulling back from her teeth. Confusion gave way to a tremor of fear as he absorbed her expression, malevolent intent plastered in thick brush strokes across her furrowed brow and burning eyes.

There was something else she spied in his expression. It was a flash of recognition that lasted a split second, and she made a mental note of it before tucking it to the back of her mind.

She retreated to the settee on the other side of the table, positioning herself with deliberate slowness before focusing her gaze on his face. Benjamin frowned as he tried to lift his arms, the handcuffs clattering behind him. The movement must have wrenched his shoulders because he emitted a drawn-out groan.

Gina allowed him time to absorb his predicament, panic inflating his chest, his breathing ragged while his eyes darted around the room. She sipped from her wine glass, the Shiraz sliding the length of her gullet, warming her insides. After struggling against his bonds, his efforts futile, he stopped moving and pinned her with a defiant gaze.

'You've made a mistake. I don't know you, lady. You've got the wrong guy. That's all I'm sayin'.'

Gina observed the bravado cloaking his posture, its paper-thin construction failing to hide his craven core. She leaned forward, noting his slight flinch and the way his gulping panic betrayed him. Without blinking, she stared him down, eyes locking with his until he looked away, his torso slumping in the chair.

'Whatcha goin' to do with me?'

Gina cocked her head. 'It's simple, really. I'm here for answers, and you're here to give them to me.' She continued, her stare locked on his. 'Spoiler alert – you're not going anywhere until you do.'

Benjamin flinched and pressed his body against the chair. His mouth gaped, and Gina leaned forward, her ear turned toward him.

'Something to say, Benji?' Gina asked in a low voice.

'Please,' the young man began, eyes wild, 'lemme go. What do ya want from me? What have I done to deserve—'

He broke off as Gina thrust her face into his, eyes flashing. 'What have you done?' she cried, spittle firing into his left eye, causing him to blink.

She continued in a calm voice, resuming her position on the couch, her erratic movements catching him off guard. *Good,* she thought. 'You're here because you are an evil, psychotic freak who kills women for kicks.'

Terror raced across his features. 'You've got the wrong person, you crazy bitch,' he spat, venom sparking his eyes.

'Is that right, hooded pecker?' she said, face cracking into a wide smile. 'Let's see if my friends were right.' She kept her eyes on his as she leaned over him, her fingers fumbling with his jeans zipper.

'Whatcha doin'?' Benjamin screeched. 'You're crazy!'

Gina paused with the zipper half-open, a crinkle appearing across her forehead. The young man's fear and humiliation were palpable . . . and unexpected. Panic bubbled in her guts, rising through her torso and up into her throat.

The man who had slaughtered Tara and the others wouldn't be fighting back tears when confronted by her scorn. No, the killer she sought didn't have the empathy to care what she thought of him and his manhood.

Doubts swirled through her mind, her pulse racing. She was trying to devise a way out of the mess she'd created when she noted the change in the man's expression. It was guilt, she thought, the flash of remorse colouring his eyes a dank grey. She watched his throat bobbing as he strove for control.

Too late for that, psycho, she mused. *You're mine now.* He knew something, and she was determined to find out what, her doubts fleeing.

'You're mine now,' she said aloud, smiling when he winced. His eyes darted, searching for an escape route. 'There's no way out,' she explained with a shrug.

She sat back on the couch and stretched one leg out before crossing it over the opposite knee. Her hands fluttered at her lap, eyes lowered, and lips parted. Anger came in waves from the man, and she braced herself.

'Bitch!' Benjamin screeched, face an apoplectic shade of red. 'Fuckin' slut! Filthy whore!'

Gina reached forward and clapped the tape across his mouth, pressing and moulding it as he thrashed his head against the back of the chair.

'No more speaking for you. Not while you continue to abuse my hospitality. In fact,' Gina said, rising to her feet with a feigned yawn, 'it's bedtime. For me at least.'

She rose to her feet and smiled at the young man, grin widening when he spat his profanities against the tape, his words incoherent. With her left hand, she stroked his stubbled cheek. 'See you in the morning, Benji. Oh, and try to get some sleep,' she added with a grin.

Crushing tiredness entered her muscles as she made her way to the bathroom. Under a stream of hot water, Gina dropped her head, shoulders slumping. Mind closed, she ran a wet cloth over her body with robotic movements.

When she opened the door to the hallway, her body encased in a thick bathrobe, the sound of music reached her ears. *I hope you enjoy Talking Heads, murderous fuck,* she mused as she retreated from the noise toward the guest room.

Huddled beneath the bed covers, exhaustion tugging at her consciousness, Gina grinned in the darkness. 'Psycho Killer' programmed to play every half hour should ensure Benjamin wouldn't sleep tonight. She expected by morning he'd be far more cooperative. At least, that was the plan.

This time, when the darkness came for her, she submitted with a beam on her face, the first since Tara had died.

CHAPTER 19

G INA WOKE TO SUNBEAMS caressing her face. She allowed herself a minute to absorb her situation. *Holy shit*, she thought incredulously, *there's a man bound and gagged in the sitting room.*

Just then, the faint strains of 'Psycho Killer' reached her. She grimaced, imagining the torturous night of no sleep and Talking Heads on repeat the man had spent.

The thought drove her from the bed to the bathroom, where she splashed water on her face, staring at her reflection. 'Who are you?' Receiving no answer, she bared her teeth, picking at a tiny remnant of yesterday's meal. 'How far are you prepared to take this?' she asked her doppelgänger.

In reply, Tara's voice drifted from her memory. At first, she couldn't place the words until she remembered the poem written by one of her patients. It came back to her in her dead girlfriend's soothing tone, every line.

> Innards yield
> Of wretched Flea.
> Tomes reveal
> In Flagellant Me
> Ancestral threads
> By woven fate,
> Prey felled in love and hate.
>
> Ink bleeds into
> Blackened ends.

Twisting regard,
Come eternal penned.
Lineage Captive,
Constrained by shame,
Offers thyself,
Shackled in blame.

'What does it mean?' she recalled asking, a chill tingling her spine.

Tara had remained staring at the ceiling, her eyes distant, troubled. After a moment, she'd glanced sideways at Gina.

'At a macro level, it speaks to the damage inflicted on a person's psyche by a catastrophic event or systemic and sustained abuse. How hatred and contempt of self can stunt emotional growth, where victims become characters in their own lives, whereby they lose self-autonomy, their tale penned by genetics and familial history. They believe their lives influenced by insidious forces that control their destiny, their story arc. It's a narrative on the cyclic nature of chaos and violence.'

She'd paused, her hand reaching to clasp Gina's arm. 'On a micro level, my patient had a father who used his body as an ashtray. Every day from age 4 till he ran away at 14, he survived physical and mental abuse the likes of which you couldn't imagine. Now, at age 41, his partner is expecting their first child, and this gentle, loving man is terrified he's going to become his father, fearing his story has been already written in genetics and he a captive to it.'

'Jesus, that's horrendous,' Gina had whispered, eyes widening as she imagined the scope of trauma that led to such a fear.

'Ink bleeds into blackened ends, twisting regard, come eternal penned,' she recited now in front of the mirror. Her eyes narrowed as she stared at herself. Had her grief and rage made her a hostage to her own story?

'How far are you prepared to take this?' Gina repeated the same question. 'To hell and back if that's what it takes,' she answered before pirouetting and retreating from the room.

She made a pit stop in the kitchen to fill a glass with water from the fridge, pausing to take a sip before she squared her shoulders and cleared her throat.

Gina approached the door to the sitting room with calm resolve. Whatever happened, she knew she was in better shape than he this morning, the final notes of 'Psycho Killer' fading into silence.

Benjamin's head hung forward, his shoulder-length hair dangling in greasy clumps over his face. Skin marred with acne, he appeared younger than his nineteen years.

'Good morning, sunshine,' she announced in a cheery voice. His head snapped back, his eyes wild. 'Did you sleep well? No? That's a shame.'

She shrugged and returned to the settee opposite him, making a show of drinking from the glass in her hand, smacking her lips together as she placed it on the table.

She stared into his fevered eyes. 'Are you going to behave yourself if I remove the tape?' She tilted her head while she scrutinised his expression flash with anger and panic before a hood drew across it. 'I'll take that as a yes,' she continued, rising to her feet. 'But I'm warning you – another outburst, and the tape goes back on, and I promise things will get a lot worse for you.'

She closed in on him and pinched the corner of tape covering his lips, tearing it free in one motion.

Benjamin winced before opening and shutting his mouth as if to test if it still worked. A strangled noise squeezed from his lips, followed by a coughing fit. His complexion reddened as the spasms continued, dry hacking filling the small space.

Gina waited for it to finish before raising the glass to her lips again. When she placed it on the table, she leaned forward. 'You thirsty?'

The young man glared back, thunder rolling across his brow. Gina held his stare, watching his resolve waver as his eyes flicked between her and the glass perched on the coffee table. He grunted and dropped his gaze.

'Not talking?' she asked, hand clasping the tumbler and moving it toward him. He glanced at her, a frown crinkling his forehead even as his eyes betrayed his desperation.

She held the glass closer until his lips parted, tipping the liquid into his mouth. As he gulped greedily, she leaned in and whispered in his ear, 'Be thankful I'm showing you more mercy than you showed your victims.'

She removed the tumbler and sat back in her seat, watching the panic race across his face before he hid it behind an icy expression. His bloodshot eyes and the rings below them told the story of his sleepless night. The flashes of fear and panic piercing his calm facade showed the effect this was having on his mental faculties. He was struggling to hold his composure. Gina smirked. Her plan was working; he couldn't hold out for much longer.

She sprang to her feet, noting the way he flinched. 'I'm going to take a shower, refresh myself. And then,' she said, her voice taking on a razor-sharp edge, 'we will talk, Benji. I want to hear all about your murdering, sick, piece-of-shit existence.' She let her words sink in, grinning when the colour flushed from his face.

Just then, the opening strains to 'Psycho Killer' sounded from the phone she'd programmed the previous night. 'Good timing,' Gina said with a laugh. 'You'll have something to listen to while I'm gone.'

With that, she reached over to reattach the tape across his mouth and turned the volume up on the song before leaving the room. Outside, she leaned against the door and exhaled. She hadn't fully appreciated the strain being in the company of the man who killed Tara would have on her. Every second, she fought the instinct to smash the glass over the man's head, to use the shards to slice his throat. She wanted him dead.

Standing under the rushing water, Gina considered again the question of how far she was prepared to go with her plan. If, when the moment came, she had the fortitude to see it through to its conclusion. By the time she was towelling herself dry, she still didn't have the answer.

As she dragged a pair of jeans over her hips and shrugged into a shirt and jumper, she pondered tactics to move the interrogation forward.

She needed to keep her behaviour erratic, unpredictability key in getting him to drop his mask, to expose the beast it hid.

To this end, when she neared the sitting room, she flung open the door and rushed toward Benjamin, whose eyes widened and flashed their rising alarm.

Without ceremony, she ripped off the tape and held the glass to his mouth again. 'Right,' she said, replacing the water on the table. 'Enough with the niceties. Time to start talking. If not . . .' She trailed off, waiting for his eyes to focus on the paring knife she held in her left hand.

'I have no qualms taking you apart in pieces,' she whispered, her voice dripping with sweetness. 'First, your fingers. Then we might keep moving, removing those bits sticking out . . . dangling.' She drew the knife forward and held its point a centimetre from his right eye.

He shifted his head to the side, a small groan escaping his lips. With deliberate slowness, she dragged the steel across his cheek to his neck, trailing it over his chest and stomach before she pressed it against his crotch.

'You wet yourself, Benji?' she asked, a grin twitching her lips. 'You stink.' Gina screwed her nostrils and pursed her lips. 'You're a feral thing,' she continued, keeping her eyes on his face, watching as anger wound its way through his fear. She kept at him. 'A disgusting excuse of a human. No way you're getting girls without force.'

The man thrust his head forward, snarling, Gina narrowly avoiding his headbutt. She raised her fist and pummelled it into his face, three sharp punches that shifted his nose to one side, blood spurting across his mouth and chin.

She left the room and returned with a cloth, which she held to his bloody face. 'I warned you. I won't take any shit. The only reason you're still breathing is because I have questions,' she continued, staring at the knife resting on the arm of the settee. 'But the next time you fight me, it won't be my fist in your face.'

Gina settled back in her seat and stared at him. 'Let's get to it.' She leaned forward, holding her mobile, swivelling it so he could see the photo of Tara she used as wallpaper. Her heart skipped when she noted

K.J. STEWART

the recognition that flashed across his eyes. It was only there for a split second, but triumph burst inside her chest.

'Lovely, isn't she?' she said in a conversational tone. 'But you know that. It's why you took her. What you don't know is how kind, funny, and intelligent she was.' She shrugged. 'You only wanted her to satisfy your own putrid, sick needs. Not me,' Gina continued. 'I wanted her for everything she was and would become. Until you took that away – her future and mine.'

She stopped, a sob clogging her throat. *No,* she mentally scolded herself, *he doesn't get my tears.* With a shake of her head, Gina reached for the knife and brought it an inch from his right eyeball. 'So ready to talk yet, Benji?'

The young man glared at her, lips pressed together. She got to her feet and stepped around the chair until she was behind him, her mouth against his ear. 'You need persuasion? Still don't think I mean business?'

In one motion, Gina grabbed his left hand, still clasped in handcuffs, and took his little finger in her fist. She bent it back until the bone cracked, the sound ripping apart the silence. He yelped, and without a word, she moved to the next digit, snapping its bone with the same lack of ceremony.

'Stop!' Benjamin bellowed. 'Please stop.'

Gina resumed her position in front of the young man, whose head fell forward, droplets of sweat falling from his lank hair. She grabbed his chin, yanking his head back until he met her eyes. He flinched, a sob wrenching from his throat, a strand of saliva clinging to his lower lip.

'How about now? Are you ready to talk?' she asked through clenched teeth. When he pursed his mouth again, she sighed. 'Have it your way.'

When she moved around the chair, he wailed. 'I can't . . . It wasn't . . . Please, no more pain,' Benjamin whimpered, the last vestiges of defiance and bravado gone.

Gina paused, eyes taking in the snivelling creature. A frown furrowed her brow. Something still wasn't right. This was not the controlled and calculated killer she'd expected, a being without conscience or remorse. Was she wrong? Had she made a mistake? Doubt flooded her chest, heart thumping while a hot tingle raced across her skin.

'It wasn't me,' the man blubbered. 'I only collected 'em.'

Gina's blood froze. She approached him, eyes searching his downturned face. 'What did you say?'

When he glanced up, his eyes were those of a trapped and tortured animal. Perspiration streamed from his pores, and his jaw clenched.

She slapped him with an open palm. 'Unless you want your remaining fingers snapped like wishbones at Christmas, answer me. What did you mean, you collected them? Collected who? The women?'

Benjamin groaned, eyes pleading with her. She struck him again. He yelped and cried harder, globules of mucus tumbling from his misshapen nostrils. When she raised her fist once more, he cried, 'Stop, stop!' His head dropped, and his sniffles became muffled.

Gina stood upright, ignoring the throbbing in her right hand which she'd used to strike him. She grabbed the glass of water and placed a hand on his shoulder. 'Here,' she said, lifting it to his mouth when he raised his head. He took a big gulp, panting when she withdrew it.

'I'm sorry,' he said, eyes begging her. 'I never wanted . . .' He trailed off when another wave of sobbing racked his torso.

Gina waited until he composed himself before leaning forward. 'You need to talk,' she said. 'I'm not stopping until I get answers, Benjamin, which means this will only get worse. I will break every bone in your body until you give me what I want. I shit you not.'

He stared into her eyes. 'Okay, okay. But first, I need to wash. I'm sittin' in piss.'

Gina considered him. 'First, you tell me what you meant. Then we'll get you cleaned.'

The young man stared with a dull expression. 'I hunted them, and I collected them. But,' he continued in a firm voice, 'I didn't kill them. You have to believe me. It was him who did it, not me.'

Gina's breath stopped while her pulse raced. Holy shit, there were two killers working together. The idea entered her brain, thoughts whirring as she tried to comprehend what he'd said. She hadn't expected this, not for one second. Nausea twisted her guts as she pictured Tara being ambushed by this snivelling creature before being taken to another, worse monster.

She rushed from the room, only just making the bathroom before her stomach heaved, expelling a stream of yellow bile. After splashing water over her face and running toothpaste across her teeth, she returned to the sitting room, where Benjamin greeted her with a tremulous cry.

'I'll talk, tell you everything,' he gushed. 'He'll hurt me, he will. But I can't . . .'

'Okay, Benjamin,' Gina spoke in a gentle voice. 'Now's your chance to get it off your chest.' She gritted her teeth. 'I can see you have a conscience,' she crooned even as her stomach clenched. 'You'll feel better once you've told me. I promise.'

She watched as the man gulped, head bobbing. 'Let's clean you up, get you more comfortable. Then,' she continued, 'you can tell me your story, which I want to hear. Okay?'

His head dipped forward, relief and tiredness settling across his face. As Gina slashed through the tape around the man's ankles, she considered the cyclic nature of life and fate. She was back where she'd been five years ago, on the brink of listening to another killer's story.

CHAPTER 20

Benjamin's Story

DAD LEFT WHEN I was little, and being the eldest, I had to look after my brothers while Mum worked two jobs. In the days, she worked in some fancy hotel in the city, cleanin' rooms for rich wankers, scrubbin' their shit from the toilets. At night, she cleaned an office buildin' in Penrith.

We lived in a shithole apartment in Blacktown, and our neighbour was this ex-soldier who didn't work. He took care of us while the old girl worked.

I was ten when he started watchin' us after school. At first, it was fun. He let me and my brothers watch TV shows Mum never did – cop shows with lots of guns and killin'. Even sex stuff.

Then he started touchin' me. First, all he did was cuddle me on his lap, which was nice. But it wasn't long before he started touchin' my junk and making me touch his.

He took me to the bedroom while the twins watched cartoons. I hated it, but I was only a kid, and it was confusing with him being so nice to us. Couldn't tell Mum, not with her working all the time. I didn't wanna add to her problems. Besides, I couldn't tell anyone what was happening. People would'a thought I liked it, that I was a fag.

The man kept doin' it for years, and I didn't say nothin' to no one. But then he started lookin' at the twins the same way, and it made me sick. I couldn't let it happen and knew there was only one way to stop him going after them. All along, I knew he wanted to fuck me, so it didn't take much till he was eatin' out of me hands. Even though it hurt, I closed my eyes, and I didn't cry, not once. When I got close, I thought of me brothers, and that stopped it.

I don't know when it changed, but I started likin' it. While the boys at school drooled over girls, I daydreamed about him in class, what we did together. I started lookin' forward to it, and that's how I knew I was a fag. As much as it made me sick, I couldn't help it.

When I was sixteen, Mum got a house from the government. It was another shithole, this time in Penrith. The man, he cried the night before we left. He told me he loved me and that he'd kill himself without me. It scared me, him talkin' like that, so I stayed with him instead of goin' back to the apartment. That's how Mum found out, when she came lookin' for me.

She went batshit crazy when she saw what was goin' on, hitting him and calling him a filthy paedo. I told her not to call the cops, that it was over, and we weren't gonna be seeing each other again. Even though she was screamin' blue murder, she didn't want any trouble, so we left, movin' into the new joint that day.

Things got better for Mum. She got rid of her cleanin' job at night and stayed home with me and my brothers. Even started smilin' again and didn't look so tired all the time.

I was glad for her, but it wasn't the same for me. School pissed me off, so I dropped out and started hangin' around the house by myself. Mum was on my back to get a job, but I felt too shit to do anything. I missed our old flat and my friends, but most of all, I wanted to see him again. If it wasn't for the promise I'd made Mum, I would have gone straight away, but after months and months, I couldn't take it, and I caught a bus to Blacktown.

When he saw me, he started blubberin' and told me he'd missed me every day. I believed him 'cause he looked like he hadn't shaved or showered or nothin' since I left. I stayed with him that night, and next mornin', he told me I could live with him, that Mum couldn't force me to go home.

She came lookin' for me two days later, but he told her I didn't wanna go home. They had a big row, both cursin' and making threats. In the end, she left. I didn't wanna hurt her, but I couldn't go home. No way was I gonna leave him again, not now I knew the twins were safe.

Since I wasn't at school and didn't work, I spent all my time with him. I found out straight off he was a druggie, and it didn't take much till I got hooked. Everything seemed okay when I was peakin', like we had no worries and me and him lived in a bubble where I wasn't a disgusting faggot. But there were problems, and after a few months, the bubble burst when the fortnightly disability payments he received from the government couldn't support our habit.

Within days of him gettin' it, it was gone, blown on drugs in the first week. We weren't eating hardly at all, and I got so thin, me ribs stuck out of me.

We got fucked up most of the time. It was the days we couldn't score that were bad. He got real angry and took it out on me. At first, he used just his fists, all the time tellin' me he was gonna kick me out, chuck me away like the garbage I was.

I was scared shitless. Last thing Mum told me was that if I stayed with him, I wasn't welcome home and that I had to stay away from me brothers. So I took it, even when he started with the belt. It had this heavy metal buckle he'd use against my backside. What was weird and kind of excitin' was it always ended with sex. It got so it was all twisted in my head, the pain and the pleasure.

One night, after a bad beating, he told me there was a way to get money for drugs, so we didn't have to go without. I said yes before he even told me his plan. I'd have agreed to anything to stop his punishments.

'You need to use what God gave ya, boy.' He had the shakes when he told me this and was pickin' at the skin on his arm.

I didn't understand what he meant at first. When he explained, I almost puked, but then I thought about the belt, and I couldn't tell him no. Besides, there wasn't another way to score, and I needed a hit as much as he did.

That first night, he came with me into Darlinghurst. He waited in a doorway while I stood on the corner, dressed in tight jeans and a singlet. At the end of autumn, it was bloody freezin', and I shivered somethin' wicked. It wasn't just the cold. I was shit scared and couldn't get my head straight. What if I couldn't go through with it? My whole body shook when I thought of the belt-down he'd give me if I turned chicken. I remember thinkin' he'd probably kill me.

So, I waited, and it wasn't long before a man in a fancy suit asked me for a blow job. I took him into an alley and sucked him off next to a rubbish bin. After, he gave me twenty bucks. I did it five times that first night, enough to score. Much as I felt dirty, like street garbage, a part of me was proud it was me who made it happen. After that, there was nothin' but the high.

I tried once, you know, to stop. Told him to shove it, that I wasn't no bum boy. It was the worst thrashin' he gave me. That buckle damn near flayed the skin off my arse. Reckon the only reason he stopped was he didn't want to damage the goods. As it was, it was a month before I could get back on the streets.

When I did, I told him I'd only do it on me own. That I couldn't do it with him watchin'. The truth was no matter how much he hurt me, I still loved him. I didn't want him to see me gettin' pumped by strangers, didn't want more shame than I already had.

That's how I came to meet . . . JD, the man you want. He saw me sellin' myself, watched me go with strangers into the alley that stank of rubbish and piss. He waited till I came back, me body achin' and head all wrong. When he came up to me, I started cryin'. I didn't wanna do it again so soon.

'Shhh,' he said. He was dressed like a teacher and wasn't like the others. 'I don't want that from you.' There was somethin' about how he said it that made me believe him.

He asked if I had a home. I told him I did. He looked at me weird like and then stared at the track marks inside me elbow. 'Is someone hurting you?'

I wanted to lie, to protect the man waitin' for me to come back with the smack. But it was as if it wasn't me who said, 'Yes.' Reckon I'd be dead if it wasn't for JD. If it wasn't for the drugs, I'd have necked myself before I even met him.

Yeah, I'd be dead, and now you're making me snitch on the person who saved me.

CHAPTER 21

GINA ROUSED HERSELF WHEN Benjamin sobbed, a strangulated cry of anguish that brought her back to the room in the mountain cottage. Not knowing what she'd expected to hear, it wasn't this story of predatory abuse of a minor.

Without a word, she stepped around the chair. Her hand reached forward, fingers hesitating at the hemline of his shirt. Dread pounded in her ears as she grasped the cotton fabric, lifting it to reveal the base of the young man's spine. He leant his torso forward until his jeans gaped to allow her a view of the tops of his buttocks. The glimpse of flesh bore out his story, a criss-cross pattern of pale scars reaching like a web above the waistband of his underwear.

Her heart ached for the young boy who fell victim to a paedophile. No one deserved such abuse. He'd gone from one predator to another, Gina pondered, shaking her head. The thought reminded her that this man took Tara, delivering her to a killer. He didn't deserve her sympathy.

Still, honey rather than vinegar seemed the best option to keep him talking. She recognised the broken child within him, the one craving attention and affection. 'I'm sorry this happened to you,' she said in a soft voice. 'No kid deserves to have their innocence and free will taken from them.'

She watched as the young man gulped back tears, his eyes glistening and softening when he met her gaze. He looked every bit the vulnerable child, and she reminded herself again that looks can deceive. He'd given up his right to clemency.

'What of your mother? Why didn't she intervene or contact the police or Family and Community Services after she left you with that man?'

Benjamin started and shook his head. 'Fewer mouths to feed. She would'a been glad to see the back of me.' Bitterness twisted his features, and his voice trembled with self-pity.

'I'm sure that's not true,' Gina exclaimed, even as she acknowledged this as a lie. How could she be certain when she'd seen first-hand the terrible injuries some parents inflicted on their own?

'What would you know?' Benjamin spat. 'Looks like you were born with a fuckin' silver spoon up your arse.'

Gina winced before fury clouded her mind. Without a word, she moved behind him and broke the little finger on his good hand, the snapping bone sounding like a starter's pistol.

Benjamin yelped and cried, and for a moment, shame crept across Gina's skin. She retrieved her seat and stared at the sobbing man, the flesh of his face red and angry, mucus dribbling across his top lip.

Once he'd composed himself, she leaned forward and spoke in a soft voice. 'Let me make this clear. You don't have a clue about me, my life. The only thing you need to understand is I have no qualms inflicting pain on you. Broken fingers will be nothing compared to what I'll do if you don't remember your manners and keep your foul-mouthed cracks to yourself.'

She watched the fear flash through his eyes and nodded, waiting until he mirrored the gesture before continuing. 'Glad we understand each other. Now let's get you that water.'

Gratitude flashed across Benjamin's face when she offered the glass to him, and a grin twitched the corners of her lips. Good – they were getting to the part she needed to hear. She was closing in on the man who'd saved him from a life of prostitution, the one responsible for Tara's death, for Jenna's and Holly's.

The thought sent a metallic taste flooding her mouth. It wasn't until she wiped a hand across her lips and it came away spotted with blood that she realised she'd bitten her tongue. She swilled a mouthful of water and dabbed at her mouth with the sleeve of her hoodie.

'Are you ready to continue?' she asked the young man, who stared at the corner of rug at his feet with vacant eyes.

'I need to piss,' Benjamin whined, his bottom lip trembling.

Gina pondered him for a moment before rising to her feet. She manoeuvred his arms over the back of the chair, ignoring his cries as his shoulders wrenched at an unnatural angle. With a shove, she drove him to his feet and out the door.

'If you're thinking of doing something stupid like trying to escape, let me remind you I have a knife I'm itching to stick in your neck,' she whispered from behind him. To lend credence to her threat, she pressed the blade into the soft flesh beneath his ear.

When they got to the bathroom, Benjamin stopped before the toilet and shook his head. 'I need me hands.'

'Allow me,' Gina stated, hiding her wince. She bit on a giggle when panic and shame flushed his complexion. 'Hey, this will be far worse for me than you. It's not as if touching stranger dick is a fantasy of mine.'

She swivelled the young man by the hips and unzipped his pants, keeping her eyes on his, enjoying watching him squirm. When she pulled forth his flaccid penis, she shook her head, forcing herself to stare at it. 'Got a decent money-maker there, Benji. You must have made a fortune on the streets.' When his eyes flashed with indignant fury, she squeezed his member in her fist. 'I wouldn't,' she hissed, lips curling.

Once he'd finished and she'd refastened his pants, she washed her hands in the sink and propelled him back to the sitting room, where she secured him to the chair.

'Okay, you've had a drink, a toilet break. So, let's get back to it,' Gina ordered from her seat, impatience sharpening her tone.

'Food,' he squawked, eyes pleading.

'After we're done . . . maybe,' she replied, tapping her wrist. 'Time's a-wasting, Benji boy. Chop-chop.'

The young man shook his head, hair swinging like a curtain across his tilted face. Gina worried for a moment he was losing it. But when he raised his eyes with a determined expression, she sighed. He was ready.

CHAPTER 22

Benjamin's Story

J D TOOK ME BACK to his house. I'd never seen anythin' like it, didn't even know people lived like that. It had four bathrooms and eight bedrooms and looked like a museum or some shit, like nobody lived there.

At first, I was goin' through withdrawals and was crook as a dog. He got me clean, sat with me while I spewed my guts out and didn't leave or belt me when I cursed at him.

He kept me in a room at the top floor until I was myself again and then moved me to a suite where I had my own bathroom and everythin'. The following months were the happiest of me life. We had this agreement where instead of payin' board, I cleaned the place, repaired stuff, and even cooked for him after he gave me a recipe book.

At night, he read from the novels he had in his library. I'd never heard anyone but teachers talk all fancy like JD. He started correcting my speech and even taught me new words. Education was a big deal to him, and I reckon I learned more from him than all them years at school.

'You won't get far in this world, Benjamin, if you don't have a firm command of the English language and can communicate with all types,' he told me. 'How can you express your thoughts, ideas, your dreams if you don't have the vocabulary?'

I didn't get everything he said, still don't, I reckon. But he didn't treat me like I was a dumb-arse, not worth pissin' on if I was on fire. With him, I believed them wrong, the ones that told me I was a loser piece of shit.

He told me I could improve myself and my 'lot in life', as he called it, just by readin' heaps. I liked spy books with secret agents who had hot bitches all over them while they saved the world. Cool as a cucumber, as Mum used to say.

But JD liked other stories. They were crime books but old ones that smelt funny. There was always ladies gettin' tortured and killed, and he loved it. He'd start breathing heavy, 'specially when the woman was tied up and strangled. That got him extra excited until he became hard.

At first, he wouldn't let me touch him. I thought that's why he saved me. Everyone wanted somethin', and no one ever did something for nothin'. But he was different.

One night, soon after I was better, I went to him. He was in bed, this big old thing with corner posts. When I came in, he was readin' one of his crime books. He put it down when I got rid of the robe I was wearin' and crawled in beside him butt naked.

'What are you doing?' he said with no feelin' in his voice. When I stopped what I was doin' and looked at him, it was the same with his eyes. I had my hand on the front of his pants, but I snatched it away when I saw them.

'Sorry,' I mumbled, all confused. It wasn't like he wasn't enjoying me touchin' him. Then I thought about the book he was readin' before I came in and realised that's what got him hard. Not me.

'Don't blame yourself, Benjamin,' he said to me when I went all red. 'This bit of awkwardness is not your fault. I am a complicated creature, to be sure. You can't give me what I need, and that is as much your responsibility as an antelope for attracting the attention of the lion.

'It's nature. Perhaps not according to the arbitrary rules written by a society hell-bent on denying man's innate instincts. They've been a part of our make-up since Cro-Magnon man stood upright and clubbed the first female he saw and dragged her into the cave to take what is his by decree of natural law.

'That so-called civilised men or cucks thought to place their own rules to govern society above those of nature's own was an exercise in arrogant, craven-hearted self-denial and a betrayal of biblical proportions.'

I can't say I understood it all but reckon I got the gist of it. The bit I didn't like was how he made me the weak one, the antelope. I didn't know how his mind worked back then, but I soon learned.

We went on after that like it didn't happen, which was best. When weeks passed and he didn't kick me out or abuse me, I felt safe for the first time I could remember.

Then one night, after readin' from one of them books, he pushed me to the floor in front of him and forced himself into my mouth till I gagged.

I felt the same as I did on the streets, comin' out of that alley. I started cryin', but he hugged me and told me he cared for me. He did it nearly every night after that, and I knew he wasn't lyin'. He really loved me.

After a while, he started talkin' about girls and how his mother was a professor at Sydney University. She was always tellin' him her students were too good for him and that he wasn't man enough to date any of them. That he was nothin' and didn't deserve the accomplished girls she taught.

One night he got real drunk on Johnnie Walker and told me about what that bitch mother did to him. After his dad left, she started lockin' him in the basement, even took out the light bulb so it was dark as shit. She left him there for hours, sometimes longer. One time, after she found him with a pair of her underwear, she kept him locked up for three days.

'I thought I'd die and decay in the blackness, my remains swallowed by the darkness until it would be like I never existed at all' he told me.

'That I'd perish in the basement and no one would know or care I was missing. Mother made sure I didn't have friends, anyone who'd know if I was alive or dead. No one to miss me.'

Any chance she got, his mother told him he wasn't a man, that he was a weakling, a soft Nancy boy. Sometimes she invited a small group of students from the uni to their house for a special dinner party. Always pretty, smart girls, the ones who were headin' places. Least that's what she told him. She shoved them in his face, paraded their fine arses in front of him, and then told him they were out of his league. That he never stood a chance with any of them.

He hated his mother, but he despised those girls more, the ones he couldn't have. It scared me, the way he raged, the veins in his neck bulging. He talked about how he'd bring them down a peg and punish them for bein' stuck-up princesses.

As for his mother, she lived in a fancy apartment in the city, near the university. She only visited him once all the time I was there, and the day she called to say she was on her way, he got real upset.

It was weird how when it was just us, he was the boss and always in control. Not after that call. He didn't act like himself, told me to leave and yelled when I said I had no place to go. 'Quit your whining, Benji. Just get the fuck out of here . . . now, before she gets here.'

I took off up the driveway and was through the main gate when I heard a car comin'. There was a bunch of trees on the side of the dirt road, so I sprinted and just made it before the car got there.

It passed in a cloud of dust, and I almost choked half to death. I thought about goin' farther into the bush and waiting it out till she left but then changed my mind. Much as I didn't wanna cause trouble for JD, I wanted to see this bitch for myself.

So I imagined I was a spy, like Jason Bourne. I went back to the house, keepin' low and using trees and bushes as cover. When I got close, I made a dash for the steps to the veranda.

There was this big window I looked through to see JD sittin' on the couch. His head was hangin', and he was wringing his hands together in his lap. I'd never seen him like this, all nervous and sweaty. He looked like a kid in trouble with the principal.

I had to move to the side to see his mother, standing over him. She was real thin, and her clothes were super fancy. Reckon her coat was worth more than all Mum's stuff put together. Her arms were folded, and she was staring at her son with disgust.

At one point, she disappeared, and when she was gone, JD raised his head. You've heard the saying about how looks can kill? Well, I reckon she'd be ten foot under if it was true. He looked like he wanted to murder her.

She stayed less than an hour. I hid in the bushes at the side of the house when she left and stayed there till it got dark. When I went back inside, I saw straight off he'd changed. It was like his mother's visit pushed him over the edge 'cause he started talkin' about the bitches that were up themselves, who thought they were better than him, Then he told me he had a job for me.

He asked me to go out and take photos on a mobile he gave me. It was pictures of women he wanted. The kind he wanted were the fancy girls who worked in the city, done up like peacocks, prancin' around in their high heels.

So I started goin' into the city once or twice a week, catching the train into Central, and each time, I returned with dozens of shots. When he looked at the photos, he went into a trance or somethin'. His favourites were the ones I took up their skirts where you could see their panties.

The videos I took gave him a huge boner, and he let me blow him while he watched. He'd talk shit, like how the bitches were so stupid, they didn't know they were bein' recorded. How they thought they were so good but were nothing but sluts and teases who all needed the same thing – a good dickin'. He enjoyed talkin' smack about them.

Then he spoke about taking one, how he'd show Mother who was good enough. I thought he was just kiddin', talking shit, until one day he said he'd bought an old courier van, so I could move around without anyone noticin'. He also told me he'd found a share house for me in Penrith, and I had to move there to put some distance between us before we did anything.

I was upset, thinkin' he didn't want me anymore, that he had the shits with me. But he told me how I was the most important person to

K.J. STEWART

him, how I was integ . . . integral to his plans and he needed me. Even when I moved into the place with the others, I still didn't know for certain what he wanted me to do. I was just happy he wasn't dumpin' me.

For two months, I lived in the house, and every mornin' I left in the van and drove into the city, just like he ordered. Every day I waited for him to text me to come to him, to show him the new photos and videos I'd taken. It was hell the days when I didn't hear from him.

I swear I still didn't know he meant it, didn't hardly listen when he said he'd ordered some drug that paralyses. I was just so happy to be with him.

One day he was watchin' one of the videos while I went down on him when he said, 'This is the one.' I ignored him, but when he'd finished, he said it again.

'Benji, darling,' he said, pullin' on his zipper, 'it's time.'

'For what?' I asked.

'Why, to take this to the next level,' he said as if it was nothin'. 'You're going to get me her.' He pointed to the frozen frame showin' one of the girls I'd seen that day.

I just stared, trying to work out what he was askin' me to do, even though in my heart, I already knew. Then he went through his plan, all the way through, and my heart went crazy. He meant it.

'What if I don't wanna do it, if I can't?' I asked.

'Well, my dear boy, then I will find someone who can,' he told me as if I was nothin'. 'You can go back to your life as a two-bit street whore if you'd prefer. Meanwhile, I'll find myself a man, not a snivelling child.'

His words cut like a knife, and all I could think was how I had no choice. I had to do it. I told him that, but he kept on about how I wasn't man enough to take one little girl for him. The way he said it made me feel small and worthless, and I begged him to let me prove myself. I told him he wasn't gonna find anyone who loved him more than me.

'Fair enough, Benjamin,' he said. 'I'll give you a chance.'

He went over his plan in detail again, and this time, I listened carefully. I had to 'cause like it or not, I was going to do this for him. I was going to collect a girl for him. That's what he called it, my job. I was the collector.

CHAPTER 23

G INA'S HEAD SNAPPED BACK, eyes drilling into the young man's face. His were half closed, a glazed expression peeking through drooping lids. It was easy to see how this pathetic, needy creature had been manipulated by this JD. She wondered if they were his real initials or an alias. Regardless, there was nothing fake about the love Benjamin bore his benefactor.

It was in his words, the tone of his voice when he spoke of him. It was the way his voice became wheedling when he explained his powerlessness that set her teeth on edge. He knew what he did was wrong, ethically and legally. Trying to weasel out from under his own culpability in the deaths that followed revealed his true self.

Rage boiled up from the pit of her stomach, and before she knew it, she aimed an open palm at his face, the slap echoing in the silence.

'Argh!' Benjamin cried, eyes wide and shocked. 'Whatcha do that for?' he implored, every inch the snivelling child.

'Don't pretend you didn't have a choice,' Gina spat, eyes flashing. 'You could have walked away and called the police, told someone what this man intended to do. Three women would still be alive if you'd had an ounce of courage. You make me sick.'

Benjamin recoiled. 'I couldn't,' he cried, tears spilling across his reddened cheeks. 'No way was I goin' back to the streets, and he would have killed me if I went to the cops. He would have talked his way out of it and made out like I was the psycho. You don't know him.'

Gina chastised herself for her lack of control. She recognised Benjamin's personality type: a needy, broken, self-pitying child able to justify his behaviour through his victim status. Bullying was not the way to extract his story, his confession. She needed more details, not the least of which was the man's name. He was the real trophy; the puppet master. This whining boy was nothing but a consolation prize.

She pulled a tissue from its box on the coffee table and wiped it across his face, coming away with smears of dirt, mucus, and tears. With a screwed nose, she tossed it to the table and glared at him, inhaling deeply to quell her anger.

The face of her phone lit up with Munce's name. She let it go to message bank, one of many she'd ignored over the past two days.

'I'm sorry I hit you,' Gina spoke in a gentle voice, watching as the young man sniffled. God, but she hated him and pitied him at the same time. That he'd been mistreated was not in doubt. He'd had a tough young life, abused, neglected, and manipulated. Still, he made the choice to throw his lot in with a psychopath, and her sympathy did not extend far enough to forgive him. Not ever.

'Why didn't he take the women himself, Benjamin?' she asked in the same soft tone, her impatience barely held in check.

The young man peered at her, eyes watchful as if on the lookout for a trap. When he didn't see one, he shook his head. 'Couldn't,' he said. 'He didn't leave the house hardly ever.'

'Why is that, do you think?' Gina enquired, eyes narrowing. She wondered how much insight Benjamin had when it came to this man. Not much, she guessed.

Benjamin shrugged, shaking his head to dislodge a dampened clump of hair stuck to his cheek. She reached to brush it aside, face reddening when he smiled. *Fuck you and your gratitude,* she thought to herself. *I just want your story – a name. Beyond that, you mean nothing to me, a flea to be squashed, exterminated.*

'Dunno,' the young man answered with a shrug. 'Somethin' to do with his mother. She was cruel, treated him like shit. Reckon she made it so he couldn't be around people, not like you mean, anyway. Maybe he used to go out a bit, like when he found me. But he didn't need to once he had me to go for him.'

Gina reclined in her chair, considering his words. He knew to a point the man was using him. He wasn't completely blind to it. This made it worse, and she ground her teeth, swallowing mouthfuls of bitter fury.

'You brought the world to him? Is that it?' she said in a strangled voice. 'At least the part that interested him, the women who angered him.'

When he dipped his head, she continued. 'And it was his mother who stoked this anger, telling him the girls she taught didn't want him, were too good for him.' She leaned forward until her face was centimetres from his. 'He used the photos and videos you took of these unsuspecting women to get off and to feed his obsession until they were no longer enough. It was then he spoke about abducting one, plucking someone from their life. Tell me, Benji, what did you think he wanted from these women?'

She couldn't keep the fury from seeping into her words. He recoiled, a hood dropping across his expression.

'Did you think he wanted to talk to them, get to know them? Woo them, even?'

Benjamin pressed his lips together, his brow drawn and eyes flitting from side to side. He wriggled in his seat, a groan escaping his throat.

'You knew, didn't you?' she continued in a steely voice. 'Even before you took the first one, you knew he wanted to harm them, kill them. Didn't you?' she screeched, rage quelling all thoughts of caution. 'Didn't you, you piece of shit, good-for-nothing murderous scum? *Right?*' she screamed into his face. 'Have it your way.' She reached behind him, fumbling for his hand as he tried to pull it away from her.

'No,' he cried, 'no more!'

She kept her eyes on his while she grasped another of his fingers in her grip and snapped it backward, the bone cracking in her fist.

'We'll be running out of fingers soon, Benji boy,' she whispered. 'Toes next? Or maybe something else, something easier for me to get hold of?' she added, eyes dropping to his crotch. She smirked when panic entered his eyes, his head thrashing from side to side. 'No? Then keep talking, Benji, and tell me what I want to know.'

His head dropped and shoulders sagged, the fight draining from his body. 'Okay,' he muttered. 'I'll tell ya what happened. Just don't hurt me anymore.'

'Fine, Benjamin. As long as you talk, I'll keep my hands to myself. You know, my hands with their fully functioning set of fingers,' she added, unable to help herself, wriggling them in front of his face.

'Good,' she said when he bowed his head without responding to her barb. 'Now go on. What happened once he got you on board as the . . . what did you call it, the collector?'

CHAPTER 24

Benjamin's Story

H E ALREADY HAD THE woman picked out, so I started plannin' how to take her. First thing was to find her again, so I returned to Central, where I'd seen her.

It took a while, but I saw her soon enough getting onto a train headin' west. She didn't even notice me get on with her, sittin' on her phone like every other fucker. When she got off at Blacktown, I followed her all the way to her house.

He was excited when I got home. Like a child, he bounced up and down, even doin' a weird dance.

'Well done, my boy,' he told me. I liked that, but then he showed me the stuff he got – chloroform to knock her out as well as the drug he found to keep her still while he did stuff. I tried to talk him out of it, I swear, but he wouldn't listen.

'Benji, lad,' he said, 'if you can't do this, don't worry. I'll find someone else to help me. There are plenty down-and-outers who'd be glad to do this small thing to show gratitude. Make no mistake – you're not the only boy out there for me.'

It was a knife in my heart to hear him talk like that, so I told him he didn't need to look for someone else. That it was me who loved him and would do this for him.

'Good, Benji,' he said, happy and smilin' again.

First thing was to find the best place to do it, to grab her. So I followed her every day for three weeks. She had a routine, and I learned it, pickin' Thursday night 'cause that's when she went for drinks after work. This meant she didn't get to Blacktown until after nine, when there weren't as many people to see.

The next week, I waited in the van one street from where she lived. I knew she passed there on the way from the station. Time moved extra slow, and it seemed like hours before her train was due. After ten minutes, I started panicking, thinking she must have missed it, and I was stressing about how to tell him I failed, when I saw her in the mirror.

My stomach was in knots when she walked near the van. I waited till she was next to it before I jumped her. It took only seconds to drag her into the van with the cloth I'd soaked in chloroform coverin' her nose and mouth. I panicked then, imaginin' someone saw and was calling the cops, so I jumped in and drove without botherin' to tie her up with the rope he gave me.

When I got to his place, he came out and opened the back of the van. He stood there for ages, just starin' at her lying unconscious, her skirt ridin' up her legs so her undies showed.

'Magnificent,' he said. 'Good job, my boy, wonderful.'

He moved aside and ordered me to carry her into the house. I put her on the couch like he said and stood back while he inspected her, pullin' on her lids to look into her eyes before runnin' his hands over her body. I was jealous but then told myself she wouldn't have been there but for me.

He pulled out a needle and got me to hold her eyelids open while he injected the stuff into the inside of the lid. It was fucked up, and I turned my head away so I didn't have to watch. When it was done, he stood over her with a weird look on his face.

'You can go now, Benji,' he said without lookin' at me as if I wasn't even there. He turned and grabbed me shoulders. 'You were wonderful, and I'm so proud of you,' he said. 'But the rest is for me. Get along to your rooms now, and I'll buzz you when I need you. Do not disturb us until then.'

I hated the way he said 'us'. It should have been me and him, not her. But I didn't wanna argue, and besides, wasn't no point in it. So, I did like he said and went to my rooms in another wing of the house.

I didn't expect it, but I slept. It must have been nerves. When the intercom buzzed, it felt as if I'd slept hardly at all. It was him, callin' me back to his rooms.

I'd sort of forgotten about the girl, so I got a shock seeing her lyin' on his bed. She was stretched out and was wearin' different clothes than the ones she had on when I took her. Her eyes were open, and she looked dead, but when I got close, they moved, and I realised she was alive. They begged me, tears in them, so I looked at JD – anything to not have to see them.

'Benjamin,' he said, his eyes on her, 'it's almost time we take our friend out of here before the sun rises.'

I looked at him, wonderin' what he meant. He couldn't be talking about lettin' her go, not when she'd run to the cops. My guts dropped, wishin' she was already dead. I thought he wanted me to do it, so when he sat on the bed beside her, I almost pissed my pants with relief.

'Hush, my darling,' he whispered to her, 'it's over now. Time to let you go, my love, my sweet.'

He picked up a pillow and put it over her face, pressin' it down and holdin' it for about five minutes. Was strange 'cause her body didn't move with the drug in her. It was so quiet and still, like there was a store dummy under the pillow, not a person.

After a while, he removed it and leaned over to kiss her forehead. I hated her, and I hated him. He didn't touch me like that, talk to me all soft and lovin'.

Before this thought was even gone, he pulled down his pyjama pants. He was hard, and he dragged me onto the bed. While forcin'

K.J. STEWART

himself into me mouth, he cradled the woman in his arms. He came quicker than he ever had.

When he was done, he ordered me to get the bag from his closet. Then he told me I had to get rid of the body. He'd done these drawings showin' how he wanted me to do it as well as a map of where to leave it.

I was still in a daze, not knowin' up from down, so I went along with it, carryin' it out to the van and loadin' it in the back along with a bag of tools.

'I'm so proud of you, my boy,' he said, lookin' into me eyes. 'Though I shouldn't be calling you that any longer. You're a man now.'

Whatever doubts I had went then. I was a man, his man, and I knew I could and would do anything he asked.

I followed the map he gave me and drove back down the mountain until I got to the national park. Lucky, it wasn't too heavy 'cause I had to carry it quite a way into the bush. I spewed into me bag after I nailed it to the tree. I was thankful I got it in the bag. He would have been pissed if I'd left DNA all over the place. Anyway, after I fixed it like he told me, I took photos, which I took back to him.

'You've made me a happy man,' he said when he saw them. I was just pleased it was over and he loved me again. Even more after what I'd done.

Next day, we saw on the news they'd found the body.

'If you did everything exactly as I instructed, they won't catch us, Benji,' he said. 'Still, we'll wait a bit before we do it again.'

I ran back to my bathroom and spewed again. It was nerves – the nails and the dead girl. And there was gonna be more. I didn't realise this was goin' to be more than just a one-off thing.

But what could I do? I was his now, and I would do anything to keep him happy, to make him mine.

CHAPTER 25

G INA EXPELLED HER BREATH, unaware she'd been holding it while
Benjamin recounted Jenna Jacklin's murder. She'd been right
when she told Munce the man who had killed these women loved
them, even romanticised a relationship. At the same time, he despised
them, a recipe for bloody chaos when you combine it with a dollop of
matriarchal abuse.

Nausea swirled in her stomach, the picture of Jenna lying on the
psychopath's bed, unable to move or fight back, swimming across
her vision. Her mind tried to stop it but couldn't, the woman's facial
features morphing into Tara's. Raw agony exploded in her chest, and
for a moment, she feared her heart would stop.

'I want his name,' she hissed at the young man, whose expression
became guarded. He appeared on the point of exhaustion, the retelling
of that murderous night sapping his waning strength.

Gina reached behind him and grabbed his hand, fingers curling
around his. 'A name – now,' she ordered, bending the first two digits
back until he yelped.

'I can't,' the young man whimpered. 'I won't betray him.'

'Hey, dipshit,' she whispered close to his ear, 'you already did. I
have you and be assured, I will find him.' She pulled back until they
were eye to eye. 'Oh, and when I do, it won't be the law with which he
has to concern himself. My punishment may be faster, but trust me, it
won't be quick enough.'

'Why?' Benjamin implored. 'Who are you? Why are you doing
this?'

Gina pondered him for a moment. 'Oh, I think you know,' she replied, scrutinising his expression. 'Tara Bennett.'

His diluted pupils told Gina everything she needed to know. Tara's death had been anything but arbitrary. It was her greatest fear confirmed, one she'd suppressed – until now. She'd been targeted because of Gina. This sick bastard had killed her to send a message to the detective pursuing him.

She watched Benjamin suck in his breath, his mouth gaping open, eyes wide. 'You knew exactly who she was before you took her,' she stated.

He flinched and dropped his gaze.

'She wasn't one of your video girls. No, he sent you to kidnap her, right? To hurt me, damage me? He wanted to show me who was in control, didn't he?'

His head shook from side to side, a sob rushing from his open mouth before his face crumbled, and he wept.

'Benji,' she spoke in a firm voice. 'You don't get to cry for her. So get your shit together and stop it,' she ordered, dropping her hands from his face.

He sniffled and groaned, his tears abating in the face of her scorn. 'I d-d-didn't,' he stuttered.

'Didn't what?' Gina said, squinting. 'You're still denying you knew her identity, who she was, who I was?'

When he didn't answer, eyes glazing over, she sighed. 'I'm going to grab myself a sandwich. Then I've got a couple of calls to make. In the meantime,' she said, leaning forward until they were inches apart, 'why don't you consider yourself, your predicament? You may not want to betray your . . . friend, but consider this – how much pain can you take? Seems to me you're not exactly the stoic type. So ask yourself, how much can I endure before this is over, before it ends?'

Her lips twitched when his eyes widened, panic infusing them. She slapped his cheeks. 'Think, Benji. It's time to consider your own fate.'

With that, she spun on her heels and left the room, the sound of his choked sobs following her through the passageway to the kitchen.

Despite what she'd told him, Gina couldn't eat, so she continued through the back doors onto the deck, mobile phone in her hand.

Her father answered on the first ring. 'Eugenia, where are you? Are you okay? You are alone, with no-one to care for you?'

Gina sighed. 'One question at a time, Papa.' She bit her bottom lip as she heard the intake of his breath. She started speaking before he had a chance to wind up again. 'I'm visiting Akeisha and Rebecca in Leura, Papa, so I'm not alone and I'm fine.' A flush spread across her throat and her face. She didn't enjoy lying to him, but it was a damn sight better than the truth. *I'm fine, just indulging in a spot of abduction and torture.*

'George, he is wanting to speak with you, but you ignore him,' Anastasios said. 'Why you are avoiding him, Eugenia?'

She sighed again and rolled her eyes. 'I'm on leave, Papa, and I don't want to talk police business. Nor do I want to speak with my boss right now.'

'And this is excuse for rudeness?' he asked, his tone straight from out of her childhood.

'Forgive me for not behaving as you want me to,' she said, bitterness clogging her airway. 'I didn't realise there was a proper way to deal with your partner being brutally murdered by a serial killer. If you've got the manual, then perhaps you could share it with me. As it is, I'm doing the best I can, but it doesn't help when others won't respect my wish for privacy.'

Gina broke off with a gasp. She couldn't remember speaking to her father as she just had. Before she could apologise, he spoke in a soft voice, as if she was indeed a child.

'My girl, my Eugenia, no one is trying to make things harder,' he said in a soft voice. 'We love you, worry for you, and when we don't hear, we think the worst.'

She reflected a moment on his words. 'What could be worse, Papa? Whatever it is, it's already happened. Tara's dead, and I'm never going to see her again, hold her . . .'

Tears strangled the rest of her words, and she brushed them away with an impatient hand. Agony clawed at her insides, and she bent double, holding the phone away from her as it took control of her limbs, her legs buckling beneath her.

The next thing she knew, Gina was sitting on the deck, knees to her chest, rocking back and forth. She had no idea how long she'd been there, how much time had passed. Through the haze of anguish, her father's voice reached her, calling her name.

She brought the phone to her ear. 'I'm here,' she croaked.

'I'm sorry,' Anastasios cried. 'I don't want to give you more suffering. Whatever you want, we will do, Eugenia. We love Tara too, miss her every day.'

Shame flamed across her face, his tears ripping through her defences. It was difficult to remember sometimes she wasn't the only one who loved Tara, who lived with her loss a visceral thing. Thoughts of her lover's family sidled from her subconscious, and she pushed them back into the far recesses of her mind. She had no room for their grief or her father's.

She shook her head. 'It's all right, Papa,' she said. 'I know you loved her too.'

They spoke for a few minutes more before ending the call. Gina hesitated, staring at the face of her phone. Her teeth gnawed on her lower lip as her finger hovered above the voicemail icon. With a fling of her hair, she pressed it, lifting the mobile to her ear.

'Hi, baby, where are you? Grab some wine on the way home, my love. You, me, a few sneaky reds in the bathtub – what do you say? Okay, gotta run, but I'll see you tonight. Bye-bye . . . Oh, and I love you . . . always.'

Gina didn't understand why she kept doing this to herself. It took a part of her every time she listened to Tara's last message. Her voice, so happy, hopeful. About what, she couldn't remember. It didn't matter. None of it did. As with the jumper, she recognised there may come a day when she'd delete it, but it wouldn't be today.

Speaking of which, she chided herself, the image of her hostage's battered features jolting her back to reality. Gina squared her shoulders and shook loose thoughts of others and obligation.

When she re-entered the sitting room, Benjamin glanced at her and moaned. She approached him and lifted the glass of water to his mouth. 'There,' she said after he'd gulped half the liquid. 'That should make it easier for you to keep talking.'

She resumed her position on the couch and peered at him with her head to the side. He didn't look stable, as if he was unravelling before her eyes. It was time to move this along, especially given her friends could return from their trip any time. Once that happened, there was no telling how long before they came to check on her.

'Time to continue with your sordid tale. Oh, and, Benji, the first time I hear you refer to the women you and your friend killed as objects, I'll hit you. Keep it up, and I'll take a piece of you. Do you hear me?' Gina grabbed his narrow chin until he met her scathing eyes. 'I need you to tell me you understand.'

He looked at her through red-rimmed eyes, resignation in the set of his jaw, the sag of his shoulders. When his head bobbed, she mirrored the gesture.

'Okay, good. So, you realised this... JD discovered a taste for killing and wanted to keep going. What happened next?'

CHAPTER 26

Benjamin's Story

THE DAYS FOLLOWIN' THAT first time were the happiest of me life. JD was kind to me. He wouldn't let me touch him or nothin', but he showed in other ways how much he loved me. One night he cooked a roast for me, whistlin' the whole time. It was nice, and for a time, I thought the nightmare had ended.

It didn't last. He started getting' fidgety and couldn't sit still. The smallest things set him off, so I had to be careful what I said or did around him. Felt like I was tiptoeing round him, tryin' not to piss him off so he'd lose it.

He'd been watchin' the news, going online to find anythin' about the woman he killed. 'They don't have a clue,' he said to me. 'I could do this every week, and they wouldn't find me. They're not smart enough to catch me. No one is.'

It scared me, him talkin' this way. I wanted nothing to do with taking more girls. It still made me sick thinkin' about the one we'd done, and I couldn't forget how she looked nailed to the tree or the sound of the nail things goin' through her bones.

'Benjamin,' he said when I tried to tell him, 'you can't go to water on me now. If you do, one anonymous tip, and the police will find you, arrest you, and you'll spend the next twenty-odd years in prison.'

I didn't know what he was sayin'. It wasn't me that killed them. But when he kept going, I knew there was no way out for me. He had me trapped.

'Do you think I'm stupid? The van is registered in your name and has your DNA all over it. Yours and the woman's.' He had this creepy-as-fuck smile on his face, which made my skin crawl. 'One call, and they'll find the van, and it's all over for you.'

The following day, I went back into the city and started takin' the photos and videos again, this time knowin' how it would end.

It took near on three weeks before he found the next. 'That's her, Benji. She's the one,' he said, pointin' to a picture of another girl who looked like the first.

When it came time for me to grab her, I was sick again, but not as bad as the first. I took her a block from her house in Emu Plains, no sweat. Halfway up the mountain, I almost shit myself when I thought she was dead. But when I checked, she was breathin', and I got her the rest of the way home.

This time, when he told me to go to me room, I didn't. I clomped up the hallway to make him think I'd left before sneakin' back to his bedroom door. By putting my eye against the crack, I could see them.

They were lyin' on the bed together, the woman on her back with JD on his side, facin' her. If I didn't know better, I'd have thought they any old married couple. I got real angry for a bit, but then I remembered the other. Even though I couldn't see this one's eyes, I pictured them open – scared and helpless.

He started talkin' to her then. It was weird, like he was having a full-on conversation with her, which only he could hear. He whispered, so I couldn't catch all of it, but what I did hear was soppy stuff, like he was in love, gigglin' like a schoolgirl. He called her 'sweetheart' and 'darling'.

'I want you to meet Mother, my darling,' he said at one point. 'Then she'll see I can get a beautiful girl like you.'

After he said that, he changed. It was like he became someone else. He leaned into the woman. 'We'll all see, won't we?' he said in this whiny, high voice, and I could see he was rubbin' himself through his pants.

So sudden it made me jump, he leapt off the bed and stood there, glarin' at her, and I saw he wasn't hard like I expected. He went over to this desk in the corner of the room. With his back to me, I couldn't see what he was doin', but I heard this snortin' noise and realised he was rackin' coke. He did three more lines, and when he turned around, he was pinchin' his nose, and I could see white powder under his nostrils. He was sniffin' like crazy when he came back to the bed and stood lookin' at the woman.

'Time to show your true colours, show everyone what's under the costume you wear, parading as if you're better, special.' He spat the last, all the while wipin' his nose with the back of his hand.

He ripped the clothes right off her. When she was naked, he stopped and stared. Seemed like forever he stayed like that, his sniffin' the only sound. Out of nowhere, he hit her, right on the side of her face. It scared the shit out of me. I think I kind of yelped, but he didn't hear.

Next, he went and did two more lines of coke, and when he came back, he had a dress in his hands. He sat on the bed next to her and grabbed her by the throat, pullin' her toward him. Then he started putted the dress on her. He was rough and was muttering real low, so I couldn't hear what he said.

I turned my head and looked along the hallway. Part of me wanted to run to my room. It was the eyes I was scared of seeing. I knew I was being a pussy, but I couldn't help it.

When I made myself look again, she was wearin' a slutty dress, and he was putting pointy-heeled shoes on her feet. When they were on, he lay next to her and started runnin' his hands all over her. He was kissin' her tits, moanin' and grunting the whole time. Couldn't see exactly, but I remembered there were teeth marks on the other and thought he was probably chewin' on this one too.

He moved down the bed, and I could see he was hard again. It reminded me of a snake striking, like a saw in a documentary at school, when he shoved his head up her dress. It seemed ages before he finished and lay back on the bed.

Feelin' sick and angry, I was gonna leave, but he started doin' somethin' I didn't expect. He moved behind her and put his arms around her, pullin' till she was half-sitting against his chest. Then he had this brush, and he started draggin' it though her hair, whisperin' in her ear and kissing her cheek. It was like she was a child and he was her father, gettin' her ready for school or somethin'.

Once he'd finished, he pulled out somethin' else. It was nail polish, and he put it on her fingernails, a bright red that shone when he held up her hand. I didn't get why he was doin' all this stuff but he looked happy, even started humming.

'There, that's better, my darling,' he said when he finished. He put his arms around her and started singing. I didn't know the song, but it was somethin' about it being a mad world, which seemed right.

I'd been trying to ignore it, but I needed to take a piss, so I crept to the toilet along the hall. When I got back, he was standing beside the bed, lookin' at her. Gone was the lovin' father or husband. Instead, he looked angry, as if she'd insulted him, hurt him. I didn't see how, seein' she couldn't speak or move.

He was shootin' fire from his eyes, and his face was red and screwed up, his fists clenched like he was gonna punch her. Then he started yelling.

'Think you're too good for me? Is that it? You're not better than me. You're not!' he cried, his face gettin' redder and redder. 'Filthy slut, prancing around like your shit doesn't stink.' He was workin' himself into a rage. I'd never seen this side of him, and I didn't know what he was gonna do next.

He moved to the end of the bed and pulled the dress up until it covered her face. 'Nothing but a two-bit whore,' he yelled, slappin' her thighs and pussy. 'Probably riddled with disease, you prick-teasing slut.'

This didn't make sense to me. One minute, she was a whore. The next, she was a tease who didn't give nothin'. But I could see there was no sense in him. He was too caught in his hatred and anger.

'I'll show you who's better!' he cried before he fell on her. He started thrustin' his cock against her undies while his teeth bit into her tits. Could see spots of blood appearin', but he was too carried away to notice.

After a while, he cried out and went stiff before he rolled off her, pantin' and sweatin'. Just as quick as the rage came, it went, and he was back to brushin' her hair where it was messed up by his thrusting.

'Shhh, darling,' he said, 'we'll get you fixed up and looking pretty again.'

It was like watchin' a storm come and go. I didn't recognise this man and was thinking about how he would kill me one day, especially if I didn't do what he wanted. At the same time, I was jealous, wantin' him to care for me the way he was her.

Next minute, I heard him snorin', so I went back to my room and got into bed. I couldn't sleep, the picture of him with the girl runnin' through me head. I must've though 'cause next I knew, the intercom buzzed, and he was callin' for me.

I don't know why, but it seemed he wanted me with him when he killed them 'cause he was waiting with the pillow again.

When she was dead, he told me to take her to the same park where I'd left the first, only in a different spot. He was certain the cops would be watching, so I had to pick somewhere else. The last thing he told me before I left was to not stop or get out of the car if I thought someone was following or watchin' me.

I did what he said and entered the bush from a different path after I was sure I was alone. It was a bit longer to walk and I had to stop heaps, but no one saw me. I almost spewed again, when I nailed her... I swallowed it this time.

After I got home, he was anxious to look at the photos I took. That's when he undid his pants and forced me onto me knees.

'I'm not waiting as long before we do the next one,' he said when I took him in my mouth. My heart fell. For some reason, I'd thought this one would be the last. It wasn't.

As I said, he'd been following the news since the first one. While he watched the daily updates, he enjoyed gloating that there wasn't a cop smart enough to find him, let alone catch him. By the time the second body was reported, he'd become obsessed with one of the detectives on his case – a woman. He read all the articles about her, including ones from years ago when she had somethin' to do with a different murder.

'This stuck-up bitch thinks she's going to catch me?' he'd yelled at the television one night. 'Afraid not, honey. I'm too smart, too invisible for you to get anywhere near me. I know your type. You waltz through life expecting everything handed to you. It's how the world works for attractive females. Then you have the nerve to cry victim, the downtrodden, held under by male boots.'

He'd ranted until his face turned beetroot red, the veins in his temple keeping beat with his words. But it wasn't until he read the background articles about this cop bein' a lezzo that he completely lost his shit.

'It's against nature, Benjamin,' he'd railed, eyes sparking like there was fire in them. 'They're traitors to their sex, to the natural order of things. These selfish bitches don't care they're going against their own biological imperative, their reason for being – to breed.'

I was frightened by his rage, but it only got worse.

'Someone needs to teach this detective bitch a lesson about what it is to be a real woman, and it's going to be me. Her,' he said, pointing to a photo posted on some online news site. It was this cop and her girlfriend, and he tapped a finger on her face. 'You're going to get her for me, Benjamin. I want to meet this Tara Bennett.'

CHAPTER 27

GINA'S STOMACH DROPPED WHEN she heard Tara's name issue from his mouth. That this man-child didn't find her by chance pitched her mind into swirling blackness. It wasn't random as it had been with the other two. They were simply in the wrong place at the wrong time, attracting the attention of a psychopath.

As she'd feared, Tara was targeted by this boy's mentor for the sole purpose of teaching her, Gina, a lesson. *Lessons,* she corrected herself, the first being she was a freak of nature and a traitor to her true purpose in life. Second, that a mere woman couldn't outsmart. *Misogynistic, murderous fuck,* she thought.

Before she knew what she was doing, the knife in her hand pressed against Benjamin's throat. Red rage clouded her vision as she applied pressure to the blade, its point piercing the skin at his Adam's apple, droplets of blood seeping from the wound.

'Under his eye, motherfucker,' Gina spat in his ear. She pressed the point of the knife harder until the droplets turned into a thin stream.

The young man let out a strangled cry. 'Please don't hurt me. I don't wanna die.'

Gina inhaled until her vision cleared. Her hand shook as she pressed the knife farther into his flesh before withdrawing it and sitting back in her seat.

'What of the women? Did they want to die?' she asked in a tone drenched in fresh agony. 'Why should I spare you, you scumbag piece of shit? What have you contributed to society other than being a parasite and an accomplice to murder?'

Gina felt her control slipping but was beyond restraint. 'You know what Tara contributed? She cared, even for leeches such as yourself. Every day she helped people struggling in their lives, in their relationships. She made the world a better place just by being in it, let alone the work she did with her patients.'

Panic filled Benjamin's eyes as they widened, staring at her. Her hands bunched into fists, and her right arm swung at him, her knuckles crunching into his cheekbone.

Without a word, she rose to her feet and strode from the room. On the other side of the door, she leaned against it. Her head rested against the timber, her breathing shallow and heartbeat erratic.

After regaining her composure, she went through to the kitchen and poured herself a glass of vodka, carrying it onto the back deck. She wondered how she was going to control herself long enough to hear the remainder of Benjamin's story.

A noise drifted across the hedge between Sylvia's cottage and next door. It was Bec's voice, and she flinched, retreating inside. She was running out of time.

With a shake of her head, she thrust out her jaw and returned to the young man, who was sobbing, his torso shaking. When he didn't respond to his name, Gina grasped his face with her hands on either cheek.

'Benjamin,' she said again, watching his eyes dart, unfocused. 'I need you to look at me.'

He groaned and tried to twist out of her grasp. She maintained her grip until he met her eyes, his fevered and pleading.

'I'm not going to hurt you again,' she said in a soft voice.

She watched his expression change, a calm falling across it. It was pitiful how eagerly the young man wanted to please her. How ripe for manipulation he was in the hands of a narcissistic sociopath. It would have been easy to turn him into an accomplice to murder.

'Benjamin, we need to hurry along. We're running out of time, and there's much I still need to know before I . . . I decide what to do with you.'

There was no need to panic the boy further, pushing him into hysteria. She exhaled and released her hold on him.

Benjamin shook his head, his drenched locks sticking to his cheeks. 'It wasn't up to me. I only did what he told me.'

Gina breathed heavily, willing herself not to stab him in the chest. 'Never mind that for now,' she said, her tone even. 'Just keep talking. What happened after he told you to get Tara?'

CHAPTER 28

Benjamin's Story

I WAITED OUTSIDE HER OFFICES until the last patient left. After twenty minutes, I figured no one else was comin', so I knocked on the door. She didn't wanna let me in. I could tell by how she looked at me. But I told her I was desperate, that I might kill myself if she didn't see me. When she turned to go inside, I shoved a rag over her mouth from behind and held on till she was unconscious.

I'd parked in the next street, so I went and got the van and backed it into the driveway. I was worried someone would see, so I rolled her in a tarp I had in the back compartment and slung her over my shoulder. It took under twenty seconds, but my heart pounded the whole time I was thinkin' someone might see and guess what I was carrying. But no one did.

There was plenty of traffic, and it took me ages to get onto the freeway heading west and another hour to reach the bottom of the mountains. I was just goin' past Springwood when I heard a noise from the back of the van, so I pulled off the highway into a side street.

When I opened the door, she was lookin' straight at me. I almost shit myself, seein' her eyes open and staring, and I couldn't move for a bit. When she spoke, her words were slurred, like she was drunk, except I knew it was the chloroform.

'Where are you taking me? You don't have to do this, you know. Let's talk before we do anything else, okay?' Her voice was calm, as if she wasn't bound in the back of a strange van. She had guts, I'll give her that.

I got up into the van beside her, thinkin' she was too out of it to escape. Next thing, she swung her body and knocked me over before falling out the back and onto the ground. I jumped after her. She had a head start, but the drug slowed her, and I caught her before she made it to the highway.

She started fightin' me, so I clocked her on the head. It wasn't hard, but it stunned her so I could get her into the van without anyone seein'. Back inside, I put more chloroform on the rag and held it over her till she was unconscious.

I didn't wanna stay there just in case someone saw and called the cops, so I drove farther up the mountain before I pulled into a rest stop. Me body was shakin' from head to toe. Cold sweat covered my skin, and I was shiverin' till my teeth rattled. My stomach churned, and I put me fingers down my throat till I vomited.

I realised I couldn't stay there, so I got behind the wheel and tried to think what to do. What I really wanted was to take her back to her offices. I was even thinkin' of somethin' I could tell him so he wouldn't kill me. Maybe if I brought him another girl, he'd forget this one. But I knew he wouldn't, and in the end, it came down to her or me.

He hurried out of the house when I got home. 'What took you so long?' he demanded, eyes blazing.

I stammered something about shitty traffic, but he wasn't listening. He opened the door and looked in, a smile spreadin' across his face. 'She's perfect.'

He made me carry her inside, straight into his room, where I laid her on the bed. I was turning to leave when he stopped me and ordered me to stay.

'What a beauty,' he said, starin' at her, his hand runnin' over her blouse and skirt. 'This one is special, Benji. A part of me wants her all to myself. However, you deserve a reward for all you've done.'

I felt sick, but I couldn't get out of it without making him angry.

'First things first,' he said, a funny look in his eyes while he opened a case beside his bed. He took out a needle and a small bottle of liquid. After he filled it, he sat on the bed beside her and told me to pull up one of her eyelids. Then he injected the stuff into the inside of her lid. I watched her eye roll, and knew she was close to wakin'.

After he was finished, he put the needle back in its box and sat next to her, with me on the other side. He slapped her face three or four times and opened her eyes. She woke up then, and she stared straight at him.

'There you are,' he said, leaning over her. 'Think you're too good for me, do you?' he went on, his expression full of hate. He slapped her again before startin' to undress her. He was in a rage when he ripped the buttons on her blouse, shoving her onto her side to remove it. When he did that, she was lookin' straight at me.

I couldn't breathe. There was this stabbing pain in me chest like I was havin' a heart attack. Her eyes begged me, but I couldn't do nothin' for her. Next second, she was on her back again. I didn't wanna look, but he made me. She was naked, and there were goosebumps all over her skin. I wanted to pull the cover over her, but he wouldn't let me.

'Bet you're not feeling so superior now,' he spoke to her as if she could answer. 'You're the same as all the others – a good-for-nothing slut, a cock-teasing temptress who looks down her nose at men. Well, your time is ending, just as it did the others. Just so you know,' he added in a whisper against her ear, 'you've got your dyke lover to thank for your being my guest. You filthy rug munchers, flaunting your unnatural lifestyle, shoving it down the rest of society's throat.'

He got up then and went to his wardrobe. When he opened it, I saw a row of dresses like the ones he put on the other two. When he came back, he got me to help get her into a short blue one which sparkled. I tried not to look at her face, but when I had to pull the dress over her head, I couldn't help but see. There were tears rollin' down her cheeks. She knew her fate and couldn't do anything to stop it.

K.J. STEWART

'Your Detective Constable Gina Palumbo,' he said. 'It's obvious she got opportunities and promotions off the backs of good officers, more deserving men. Typical in this PC world, this topsy-turvy dimension where the majority pander to the minorities, everyone too scared to tell it how it is for fear of offending someone. Well, not anymore, not here,' he spat, getting himself more and more riled. 'You and your Gina need to learn an important lesson, and guess what? Class is in session, sweetheart.'

I couldn't get the image of her eyes out of my mind, and I started cryin' myself then, couldn't help it. That's when he tipped over the edge.

'Instead of blubbering,' he said in a tight voice, 'make yourself useful, Benji, and open her legs for me.'

I shook my head. 'I-I-I don' . . . I can't,' I said. 'Please don't make me. I wanna go to me room.'

He looked at me, eyes like stone. 'It's my room,' he said, 'not me room,' as if the real problem was my bad English.

'Please,' I begged, 'let me go to me . . . my room. I'll take her when you're done, like I did the others, but I can't do this, please.'

He beat me. With steely eyes, he took his belt off and thrashed me with it on me back and legs. He only stopped when I begged. Then he jumped on her, bitin' all over her neck and tits, rubbing himself against her till he blew.

'Now, Benji,' he said when he was finished, 'are you going to behave and help me?'

My wounds burning with pain, I couldn't speak, so I nodded instead. Truth was, as much as I was afraid of him and what he would do if I refused, I still loved him. He'd become my whole world, and without him, I had nothin'. For that, for him, I knew I'd have to get through what came next, do what he asked, and get rid of her once he finished.

CHAPTER 29

EARS STREAMED DOWN GINA'S face. Listening to this creature
describe Tara's last hours crushed every part of her. A rage-fuelled
bellow bounced off the sitting-room walls as she lashed out, striking
the boy's face with a clenched fist. The impact sent his head rocketing
against the back of his chair, blood seeping from the corner of his
mouth. She stared at the crimson rivulet as it traced the curve of his
chin.

Without knowing how it got there, she raised the knife to his throat,
his Adam's apple bobbing as if trying to escape the deadly blade.

'How fucking dare you imply remorse?' she spat, fury overtaking
her thoughts. 'You had the chance to stop this madness, but you didn't.'

She continued when he shook his head, snot dislodged by the action
flying across the room. 'No, no, Benji, no more excuses. You could have
saved her, saved Tara . . .'

Gina's voice broke, and she pressed the tip of the blade against
his flesh, ignoring his yelp when it broke through, a stream of blood
staining the neckline of his shirt.

'Please stop,' he implored, his words strained with his head tilted
back against the chair. 'He hurt me, beat me. I couldn't help her.'

She released the pressure on his throat, and with deft movements,
she circled him, pulling up the shirt to expose his back to her gaze.
There were cuts and bruises, the latter yellowed with age, criss-crossing
his spine. They stretched between his shoulder blades, which poked
through his flesh.

'See? I'm not lyin',' Benjamin beseeched before he resumed snivelling.

Gina returned to stand in front of him, staring at his splotched and red-pocked face. *Pitiable*, she thought. He was nothing but a marionette under the control of a psychotic puppeteer.

'What's his name?' she asked, head to the side and eyes narrowed. 'Who is this beast who beat you, who killed innocent women?'

Benji stopped crying, a veil falling across his expression. He shook his head, and Gina's hands curled into fists. She inhaled a shaky breath.

'What have you got to lose?' she continued, keeping her focus on his eyes, noting the panic flashing through them. 'It's not as if you're getting out of here. You get that, don't you, Ben—'

A knock at the front door interrupted her.

Benjamin opened his mouth, and she clamped a hand across his lips, cutting him off mid-cry. She flung her head to either side until she spotted the tape she'd removed that morning. With one motion, she withdrew her hand and replaced it with the tape, pressing against it to make sure it held firm.

Gina glanced down at herself, brushing her hands against her jeans and straightening her shoulders. She planted a grin on her face as she approached the door, swinging it open to find Rebecca on the other side.

'Hey, Gee,' her friend said, a frown creasing her forehead. 'We're back from our trip. Is everything okay here? I thought I heard a noise.'

Gina strained to keep her smile intact, head shaking. 'Hm, I don't know,' she said. 'It might have been the television.'

Moments passed in silence as Bec scrutinised her, eyes wandering over her, lingering on her hands, which she pushed behind her.

'What did you do to your knuckles?' Bec asked, reaching to grasp Gina's arm. The latter jerked away and then laughed, a forced expulsion that fell between them.

'Just some gardening,' she said with a wave. 'It's nothing. So how was your trip?' she asked, hoping to divert her friend's attention.

Bec stared at her for a moment before replying, clearly not buying her explanation. 'It was great. We spent a day with Robin and Tom plus their little rug rats. It was fun, but I'm not here to talk about the trip.'

'Oh?' Gina said, swallowing the panic balled in her throat.

'I'm here at the behest of George,' she continued, eyes narrowing. 'He told us he's been having trouble reaching you. You're not returning his calls.'

Gina shrugged, a gesture that caused her friend's frown to deepen. She sighed. 'I don't want to speak with him.'

'Why not? I thought you'd be all over the investigation.'

'Bec, I don't want to talk to anyone. I'm not sure how much clearer I need to be on this.' Gina broke off with a shake of her head. 'I'm sorry,' she said, shame flushing her complexion. 'I don't mean to be rude, and I appreciate you and Akeisha lending me this place for a bit. But I'm not strong now. Not enough to follow the investigation. It's the whole damn reason for taking leave from work. I can't handle it.'

Rebecca pondered her with a grunt, her head on an angle. 'Is there anything you need?'

Gina hid her smirk, relief washing through her. She shook her head and grinned. 'I'm fine. You guys stocked me with everything I could possibly need. Thank you so much. But for now, I'm better off by myself.'

Bec scanned Gina's face. 'Okay, Gee, I'll leave . . . for now. Just remember Keish and I are just next door if you need us.'

'Thanks, Bec. I appreciate it.'

'I do need to get back to George,' Bec stated with a stern expression. 'What do you want me to tell him?'

Gina pondered the question before replying. 'Tell him I'm fine. That I'll be in touch with him soon, I promise.'

'Okay, will do,' Bec replied. She pursed her lips before grasping Gina by the arms and pulling her against her chest. 'I love you, woman,' she whispered.

'Me too,' Gina replied, choking on a sob. 'Go,' she said, pulling away from her friend. 'I've got a date with the couch and the new Scarlett Johansson movie.'

Bec laughed. 'Fair enough. Enjoy, and I'll check in with you tomorrow.'

Gina waited on the porch until her friend disappeared beyond the curve in the driveway. She paused and breathed in the damp air. A light mist swirled across the landscape, wisps that wound through the hair at her nape, causing her to shiver.

She wasn't comfortable lying to her friends. Hell, she'd stolen their vehicle and used it in the execution of a crime – or several – so what difference would a lie make to her rap sheet?

Besides, it would be over soon, she thought. The idea brought a shadow across her mind. She'd lost sight of her endgame. Twenty-four hours ago, she had believed in her plan for Benjamin. That was before she'd discovered his role in the women's deaths. The fact that he was the accomplice to the true monster had shocked her. Now she hadn't a clue what she was going to do with the young man. The only thing for certain was this older man, this murderer, must face justice and punishment, and if she had her way, it would be by her hand.

She squared her shoulders and ground her teeth at the thought of this unidentified sociopath, the one Benjamin called JD. It was time to draw his true name from the man inside. She entered the cottage with a determined stride.

He sat as before, head slumped, hair knotted and bedraggled against his face. She noted with shame an acrid odour, his crotch wet with urine. Conflicting emotions raced through her. On the one hand, the young man's story had touched a part of her she'd almost forgotten since her time with Sylvia in this cottage. He too had a rough childhood, which had impacted on his psyche in ways she barely understood. Tara would have, she thought, bitterness chasing away any burgeoning empathy she had for him.

No, he was still responsible, in part, for her lover's demise and, as such, deserved the punishment she wrought. She left the room and went to the linen closet, from which she grabbed a towel, returning to the sitting room. With hesitation, she approached Benjamin and held the towel over his crotch, dabbing at the wet patch with her head averted.

'There,' she said, 'that's a little better. Not long now, Benji, and this will be over, but first, I need the name of the man you say you love. You know, the one who beat you, used you, threatened to make you the scapegoat for his crimes.' Gina paused and placed a hand under his chin, lifting his head until he met her stare. 'Is this a man deserving of your protection? You say he loves you, but that's bullshit. I think deep down, you know this.'

Benjamin flung his head back with a snarl. 'No!' he wailed. 'You're wrong. He loves me. You don't know shit, bitch.'

Gina snapped. She struck him in the face and kept punching while he screeched, flinging obscenities at her. Savage rage drenched her vision a mindless red, driving her fists into him again and again until blood spurted from his mangled nose, his right eye swelling and closing.

With a wrenching sob, Gina stopped, her hands covering her face. 'Shit!' she cried, her knuckles bloody and raw. She stared at them and then at the weeping man. He stared from his good eye before firing a globule of blood-filled spittle at her right cheek.

She froze, his saliva tracing the curve of her face. Her fury morphed into cold rage, and she stormed from the room without a word. At the bathroom sink, she stared at her reflection in the mirror. With robotic movements, she reached for the wash cloth and patted her face, wiping the spittle from her. Her eyes held a haunted expression, agony and grief shimmering through her tears.

Gina stood as minutes ticked by, unable to move, to think. She waited until her anguish eased and her eyes dried. *Right,* she thought, *time to end this.* She couldn't handle much more of this, not without losing more of herself than she already had.

When she next peered at herself, she gasped. Tara stood over her right shoulder, her image shimmering against the reflective surface. She glowed, and Gina clasped a hand across her mouth to hold back a scream – or sob; she didn't know which.

'Tara,' she whispered, the word warming her palms for a moment. A single tear tumbled over her lid, and she blinked, scared that in the microsecond her eyes closed Tara would disappear.

She was still there, an expression of compassion and understanding softening her features. The ache in Gina's chest expanded, filling every part of her.

With a trembling hand, she reached her fingers to brush the mirror where Tara stood, terrified the image would explode beneath her touch.

K.J. STEWART

At the same time, she couldn't stop herself. She expelled a gush of breath when it remained intact, vivid.

'Tara,' she said, the name an incantation. She hoped that repeating it would hold the visage together. With a shake of her head, she admonished herself. It was an impossible dream. A fantasy which didn't belong to this place, in this time.

'You're dead,' she hissed through clenched teeth. 'The man who was part of that is here, and you're not. You don't get a say in how I survive your loss, you hear me?' Gina shrieked, hand wiping angry tears from her face.

With a final smile filled with sadness and resignation, the image of Tara faded until it disappeared.

With a sigh, Gina placed her hands on the vanity top, breathing to calm herself. She straightened, the muscles in her shoulders screaming. Groaning, she pivoted and walked through the kitchen toward the sitting room.

She clenched her teeth at the door, steeling herself before she entered. When she entered the room, the expression on Benjamin's face sent icy shock waves through her.

He smiled, a macabre sight among the wreckage of his features. 'Ya said he didn't love me,' he slurred through his bruised and sagging jaw. 'I knew he'd find me. Now you're goin' to get it.'

Gina's mind reeled, trying to keep up with what he was saying. *How could this be?*

'Holden was right, you're not as smart as you think you are,' Benjamin sneered. 'All you need to track someone is a mobile.' He broke off with a cackle that raised the hairs on her arms.

Her stomach plummeted into her shoes as her eyes darted around the room. The phone sat on the mantle, right where she'd put it when she first tied him to the chair. She'd made a terrible mistake. *Lord, please don't let it be my last,* she prayed.

Just then, the lights went out, plunging the room into shadowy gloom.

CHAPTER 30

Gina's heart pounded against her chest, her eyes darting in search of the unseen presence. She perceived the room as empty but for Benjamin and his unhinged laughter.

She looked around for her own phone, heart sinking when she recalled leaving it on the kitchen bench after speaking with her father. The knife she'd held against the young man's throat was no longer on the coffee table, and panic swelled in her chest. An image filled her vision, of herself striding from the room after cutting Benjamin. She could see the hilt of it clutched in her fist. The picture only lasted a second, before it split apart. She had no idea what she'd done with it from there.

Her breathing shallow and pulse racing, she fought the rising hysteria in her gullet. She had to move. Whoever cut the electricity was somewhere inside the cottage, and she had to find him before he found her.

She pivoted and faced the open doorway. By increments, she eased her head around it until she could see into the front foyer. Shadows played against the walls, lending the space an illusion of movement. She glanced at the front door, itching to take flight. But she needed her phone, the compulsion to call Munce driving her actions.

Gina inhaled before she edged into the foyer. She crept on silent feet, her left shoulder brushing the wall. A few more steps, and she'd reach the kitchen. But where was he?

Just as she reached the entrance, a draught fluttered the hair at her nape. As she twisted, something sharp pricked the skin below her ear. Instinctively, she swivelled her head, breaking contact with the alien object. With a violent jerk, she flung her arm backward with a clenched fist. A wave of satisfaction flooded her when she heard the crunch of nose cartilage. The man grunted, stepping away from her.

Gina took the opportunity and sidestepped him, a shadowy figure with features glowing in half-light. Heart hammering, she raced for the front door. Flinging it open, she stumbled on the front-porch stairs, pulse drumming in her ear. With one leap, she took the last two steps, landing on the driveway with a jolt. Her legs pumped as she ran, her breathing heavy, adrenaline propelling her to greater speed.

She didn't detect any pursuit as she surged along the driveway. At the curve, she lost her footing on loose gravel and slipped to the side, her body crashing and sliding to a halt. She yelped, pain shooting through her palms and knees. With a cry, she pushed herself from the ground and continued in a limping gallop until a flash of white caught her eye.

She skidded to a stop, sending small pebbles scattering. A lady's sand shoe protruded from a gap between the lavender bushes lining the driveway. Terror gripped her as she approached the still figure it belonged to.

'No!' she cried. 'Bec. Oh, Bec, please be alive.'

Her friend lay on her side with no outward sign of injury. Gina forced herself into action, coming to rest on her haunches beside her. With trembling fingers, she placed them against the side of Bec's throat, letting forth a sob when she detected a pulse. It was faint but there. She was alive.

Gina manoeuvred Rebecca onto her back and gasped. Her friend stared back at her through terrified eyes.

'Oh fuck, Bec, what's he done to you?' she cried. She grasped her friend's arm, tugging until her torso lifted from the ground. When her head lolled back, she eased Bec to the ground and sobbed. 'He got you.'

The sound of a slamming door reached her, and she clambered to her feet. She chewed her bottom lip, assessing her options. Her friend needed protection in her incapacitated state, so she had to lead him away from her, so she made a split-second decision.

'I'll be back,' she told Bec, whose eyes mirrored her own alarm.

Gina took off, legs straining as she retraced her steps toward the cottage. At the bend, she saw the figure on the front porch. His back was to her, so she willed herself to greater speed, sprinting to the side of the house.

She heard him coming after her as she pounded along the overgrown path. When it opened at the rear, she panted as she raced onto the first level of the garden. At the steps, she launched herself from the top, ignoring the jarring through her knees as she landed. She dared a glance behind, heart tripping to see him gaining on her.

Gina veered to the left, along the track leading to Sylvia's apple tree. She glanced at it as she wheeled to the right into a copse of trees. By now, the sun was starting its descent, and fog rolled in from the gorge. It cloaked her from view as she rounded the trunk of a large oak, crawling and huddling against it.

From her position, she could see the hedge dividing the property from next door, where Akeisha was no doubt wondering what was keeping her girlfriend.

'Please don't come over to check,' Gina mouthed. 'Stay where you are.'

She could no longer hear the man in pursuit, which only increased her anxiety. Fear he'd burst from the trees pinned her to the rough bark. To distract herself, she traced the hedge until she spied the gap through which she'd first gazed upon Sylvia performing her harvest dance.

The idea that she'd come full circle invaded Gina's brain, and she clasped a hand across her mouth to stifle her hysteria. *If only Sylvia was here now*, she mused, the idea soothing her.

The snap of a twig catapulted her back to her current predicament, and she craned her neck to peer into the opening with the apple tree. The fog was thicker, and she strained her eyes, head shaking. Something was wrong. The corners of her vision blurred, objects morphing and melding into colours without shape.

As she stepped forward with a measured tread, panic filled her mouth till she thought she'd scream. Her legs wobbled, their heaviness alien. Nausea clawed at her insides, and she stopped, clasping a hand over her mouth. Her skin felt clammy, rivulets of perspiration pooling against her splayed fingers.

Gina reached to touch her neck, her finger tracing the tiny mark where the hypodermic had pierced her skin. She thought her counterattack had blocked the flow of liquid, but it seemed an amount had entered her bloodstream.

Fuck! The voiceless scream came as she swayed on her feet, bending double to grasp her knees. She steadied herself, gulping in the heavy air.

Another noise reached through Gina's confusion. She narrowed her eyes, ignoring her frayed peripheral vision. There, near the apple tree.

The silhouette of a tall man of thin build appeared through the mist. The copse of trees hid her from his view, and she forced herself to stillness, concentrating on tracking his movements.

Another wave of dizziness knocked against her, and her legs faltered, pitching her forward. When she placed a foot to keep balance, it disturbed a pile of maple leaves, the crunching noise enormous in the still air.

The man's head snapped toward where Gina cowered. She leapt up, mind screaming at her to run, her legs fighting the paralysing drug to obey.

The crashing noise of pursuit sent terror through her as she focused on the path leading to open garden and the stairs to the lowest level. She reeled to the side, her limbs struggling to receive messages from her brain.

A yelp escaped her lips when a hand brushed her shoulder, fingers scrabbling at the fabric of her hoodie. With a jerk to the right, she pumped her legs harder, eyes on the steps coming at her fast. At the top landing, she sprang into space, landing with a jerk that rattled her knees, bringing them out from under her.

She sprawled to the wet earth, her breath expelling in a violent whoosh. Clasping her side, she pushed upright and ran. A scream wrenched from her throat as her head snapped back, bringing her to a skidding halt. She fought for balance, pulling her head forward, the clump of hair in the man's fist ripping from her scalp with a wet sound.

Gina yelled in agony and anger as it came free. She leapt forward, the killer at her heels. In her mind, she counted. *One, two, three.* He was right behind her now. His breath came in heavy blasts. *Four, five, six, seven – almost there.*

She braced herself, skidding and slipping as she battled her momentum. She flung herself to the right, bracing herself for impact. It never came. A hand grappled with her shoulder, fingers digging into her collarbone, wrenching her toward the figure teetering at the edge of the cliff.

She whipped her head and found herself eye to eye with the killer. His head was turned to stare at her with a mixture of hatred and fear. One hand clamped onto her, while the other flailed mid-air, the man's torso bending toward the empty chasm while his feet scrabbled to find a foothold.

It was like it was happening in slow motion, his hold pulling her toward the lip of earth, her legs straining against him. She realised in that second that gravity would take them both, sending their bodies to break against the rocks and trees below, and all she had to do was let it. The thought brought with it peace. She'd have him. Even if she lost her own life, she'd take him with her. So be it. It was enough for her.

'Drop now!' a voice bellowed in her ear.

In one violent motion, she flung herself backward, her legs slipping from underneath her as the killer kept his hold on her hoodie. She flipped onto her stomach, groaning as the man held on, his grip like a vice. Her fingers scrabbled, digging into the wet dirt. Behind her, a yell tore through the air, and she whipped her head to see a flash of grey disappear over the cliff edge.

Gina felt the grip on her jacket slip as the man fell. She sighed, a sound broken off when fingers grasped her ankle, which dangled over the earth's lip. At once, her body lurched across the ground, the man's weight dragging her toward the precipice.

She screamed a hoarse cry, hands flailing, clawing at the earth, desperate to find an anchor. Her legs now dangled into space, only her torso on firm ground. At last, as she slipped closer and closer to the edge, her fingers grasped something solid. Agony tore through her arms and shoulders as her momentum stopped, the killer's weight wrenching her muscles.

'Argh!' she cried, pain exploding through her as she strained to keep her grip. She panted, her tendons screeching. It was no good. The man was too heavy, and she couldn't hold on for much longer.

'Think,' the same voice who'd yelled at her before spoke in her ear. 'You know what to do.'

Of course, she admonished herself. She wasn't a helpless victim. For fuck's sake, she was Tara's warrior goddamn princess.

With that, she focused on her legs, testing which held the man's weight. She willed her brain to deliver the message to the free one, which she raised, bending it at the knee. With all her force, she drove it downward, sensing rather than feeling her shoe connect with the killer's arm.

A cry of pain and fear confirmed she'd hit her target. She brought it down again and again until a wail split the air above the gorge, a terrified bellow cut off with thudding abruptness.

The blood in Gina's veins froze. Loose gravel tumbling over the lip of the gorge on either side of her aching fingers brought her back to herself. With a grunt, she dragged herself until she rested on solid ground.

She flopped onto her back, groaning even though she felt no pain. The narcotic had reached her nervous system, making her limbs outliers to her consciousness.

Gina couldn't move, and tears rolled from the corners of her eyes, tracing flesh now numb. Was this it for her? *Fitting*, she mused. At least, she'd taken the murdering bastard with her, the thought bringing her peace as she surrendered to her fate.

CHAPTER 31

Gina blinked as a finger of light pierced her retina. Her head felt stuffed with gravel, which grated against her skull when she tried to lift it. A hand pressed against her shoulder until she slumped back against the ground. The dank earth and frost nipping at her fingertips confirmed she was still outdoors – and alive.

'Can you hear me, Detective Palumbo?' A deep voice penetrated her throbbing temple.

'Wha . . .' she slurred, her swollen tongue filling her mouth.

Try as she might, Gina couldn't discern where she was nor why her head was surely twice its usual size, her limbs wooden. *But I'm a real girl,* she mused, hysteria nipping at the frayed edges of her mind. To add to her disorientation, she didn't recognise the voice of the figure who came in and out of focus.

'You'll be fine,' the person continued in a soothing tone that did little to quell her swelling panic.

Something had happened. She blinked tears that spilled across her cheeks. If only she remembered, this confusion would end. She concentrated on the person with the kind voice.

'Tara,' Gina croaked. 'I want Tara.'

'Detective Palumbo.' The faceless stranger had one hand resting on her shoulder. A beam of light struck first one retina and then the other. 'Inspector Munce is on his way. He should be here any minute.'

At mention of her superior, a moan started in Gina's narrowed throat. It cloaked the wail snarling and gnashing at her insides, ripping her apart. It came back to her in a tsunami of agony and grief. Tara was dead, murdered.

The aftermath of her death flashed through her mind, images of Benjamin's closed eye and battered face making her cringe. Had she done that? Then came the man, the true puppeteer and monster who'd chased her through the garden.

Gina's head snapped forward, eyes wide. 'The man.' She panted from the exertion of trying to sit. 'He went over . . .' She brushed aside the hand covered in coarse black hair from her arm. 'The edge,' she cried. 'The gorge . . .'

'Shhh, you need to take it easy, Detective,' the man said, his face coming into focus, expression grave. 'You're still under the influence of a strong opiate. It'll be a few hours yet before it leaves your system.'

'Opiate?' Gina said, brow furrowing. She gasped. 'The needle . . . It got me?'

'A small dose, yes,' the man replied, his fingers resting against the side of her neck, measuring her pulse. Next, he strapped a blood-pressure monitor to her arm.

Gina swivelled her head to peer about her. Blurry figures stepped through swirling lights, and she closed her eyes as trepidation filled her. It seemed she remained under the influence of a powerful narcotic. But when she looked again, she realised it was the fog that distorted her vision.

The nebulous shroud covered the scene, but she could still make out the nearby table and bird feeders belonging to the lowest tier of Sylvia's garden. She wondered whether the dead woman's birds understood their patron would never return.

She couldn't discern the number of figures crawling across the garden. She recognised police uniforms and those of search and rescue. Then there was her carer who was kitted out in a paramedic's uniform. It seemed this party was open to everyone.

A memory pierced her brain, bringing with it a wince that reverberated through her chest. 'Where's Rebecca? Did you find her? Is she okay?'

The man removed the monitor from her arm and patted her hand. 'We found her, and she will be fine. She's your friend?' he asked with a smile which reached his ridiculously blue eyes. If she swung that way, she'd be swooning right now.

'Yes,' she rasped. 'Where is she?'

'We found her first and got her stabilised before sending her on to Nepean Hospital. Her girlfriend accompanied her, so there's no need for you to worry.'

Gina's lips twitched, and she inhaled, relief sweeping through her. Bec was fine. No doubt experiencing the same grogginess as she.

'You'll be following shortly,' the man continued. 'You'd be there already except DI Munce wanted you treated at the scene until he gets here.'

'Oh,' Gina whispered, aware now of an aching which spread through her arms and into her shoulders. It wasn't just the pain that had caused her to wince but also the thought of Munce's anger and disappointment. She'd gone rogue, ignoring and disrespecting her training, his authority, and the department.

As if she'd conjured him, Munce's voice reached her. A moment later, he knelt beside her, his face hovering inches from hers. He met her eyes before facing the medic taking care of her.

'What's her status?' he asked in a gruff voice.

Gina didn't listen to the man's reply as she scanned her superior's features, trying to assess the level of his fury.

'How are you feeling?' he addressed her, his words clipped and professional.

'I'm okay, sir,' she said in a low voice. 'Sir, I'm sorry. I-I . . .' She broke off when he raised a hand.

'Not now, Detective,' he ordered. 'In fact, I'd recommend against speaking to anyone. Do you understand . . . Gina?'

At her name, she blinked, realisation breaking through her tangled thoughts. He was trying to protect her. Relief and shame waged a battle. He shouldn't be in this position and wouldn't be but for her and her single-minded thirst for revenge.

'Where's Benjamin?' she asked, flinching as his gaze hardened. 'The boy – is he in custody? He was . . .' Gina trailed off when Munce shook his head.

K.J. STEWART

'Dead,' he said, eyes boring into her.

Gina's mind struggled to comprehend. 'What? How?' she cried in a high-pitched voice. She swallowed before the hysteria erupted and made things worse. She sensed they weren't great as it stood.

The inspector tilted his head as he studied her. He remained silent, his stare heavy against her chest.

'I didn't . . .' Understanding dawned, and she gasped. 'It wasn't me, sir. I didn't kill him. You have to believe me.'

Munce pursed his lips, scowling until his eyebrows touched. When he still didn't speak, Gina's heart raced, fear covering her in a sheen of prickling sweat.

'Oh god,' she groaned, nausea flipping her empty stomach. 'I get how it looks,' she said in a voice she forced to calmness. 'There was another man, sir. I swear. He's the one who attacked Bec and came after me. He must have killed Benjamin.'

She broke off, eyes meeting his. Gina forced herself to hold his gaze, to withstand his scrutiny with unflinching stoicism. She recognised his stare as an interrogation technique, but this was the first time on the receiving end, and she didn't enjoy it. She understood why criminals cracked under the stress. He represented and epitomised every authority figure she'd ever encountered, their judgement and scepticism, their disappointment. It was soul-destroying.

Munce's head dropped into a curt bob, and he averted his gaze. Gina slumped, exhausted. She blinked and frowned when he looked at her again, his brow still drawn.

'He was banged up,' he said, eyes narrowing. 'What do you know of that?'

Images flashed across her vision. Benjamin's open-mouthed scream as she broke the bones in his fingers. She couldn't remember how many. The sound her fists made when they shattered his nose played like a demented symphony against her eardrums.

She flinched, meeting Munce's eyes. He sighed, one hand curling around his top lip to cover his mouth.

'Right,' he said brusquely. 'Enough said . . . for now.' He reached out and brushed a strand of hair from her cheek, tucking it behind her ear. 'Why didn't you talk to me?' Munce asked, the shimmer of tears driving a dagger through Gina's breast. It was worse than his silent condemnation.

A dam burst, unspent grief erupting into a wail that wrought the night air. 'I'm sorry,' Gina cried while he lifted her into his embrace. 'Sorry,' she repeated, the only word she could manage. 'Tara!' She screamed the name over and over, agony thrashing her torso, pitching it into fits.

She clung to George's solidity, his barrel chest her life raft as anguish tugged at her, drowning her. Time stood still until she fell into hiccupping sobs, her throat hoarse and eyes burned dry.

Gina returned to herself and the present in gulping starts. Exhaustion gripped her limbs, but she fought it to sit upright, breaking free from Munce's arms. He peered into her eyes before smiling, a tentative twitch which spread into a wary grin.

'George,' she whispered, 'take me inside, please. I need to see him for myself.'

CHAPTER 32

I T TOOK CONSIDERABLY LONGER to retrace her steps to Sylvia's cottage than her earlier wild flight. Munce supported Gina as they made their way to the rear deck. Inside, she hesitated, wincing beneath the stares from the officers filling every corner.

Inspector Munce squeezed her elbow and nudged her forward. They walked past the kitchen and into the hallway leading to the front entrance. He leaned her against the door frame to the sitting room while he entered, ordering everyone to leave. Gina kept her gaze downturned as figures pushed past her, the room emptying until just she and Munce remained.

With a thudding heart, she hobbled on wobbly legs toward the boy slumped in the chair where she'd left him. A tic began in her temple as she breathed in and out until composure settled across her mind. She raised her eyes.

A gasp pushed through her clogged throat. There was so much blood. It covered his neck where the ends of a vicious incision split the flesh from ear to ear. Munce raised the young man's head by clasping a thatch of auburn hair in his gloved fingers. The wound split into an obscene grin, and Gina noted the killing stroke went through to the bone. Death would have come quickly, but she guessed not swiftly enough for Benjamin, who would have drowned in his own blood.

Her stomach churned, yet she couldn't take her eyes from the gaping flesh. The flow had dried, meaning Benjamin had died hours earlier.

Gina then scrutinised his face: the blackened and closed left eye, the red smear under his nose, the cartilage off-centre where her fist had slammed into it again and again. Shame washed through her, and she groaned. Standing with Munce, it was as if another person had inflicted this tapestry of wounds, including the broken fingers still held in handcuffs against the back of the chair.

Munce rested a hand on her shoulder as her hand covered her mouth, bile filling it until she had to swallow to stop it spilling.

'I'm sorry,' she whispered, not knowing whether it was meant for the boy or Munce.

Gina's mind replayed the last moment she saw him, the ghoulish grin on his face when he believed his lover had come to rescue him. She remembered edging from the room, the breeze that forecast the man's presence, the needle slicing into the side of her throat. Then running from the cottage, finding Bec sprawled in the garden, her eyes alive while her body lay as if dead. A shiver traversed her spine, sending tingles through her extremities.

'The other – he must have killed Benjamin when I ran out the front door. I wondered why it was a few minutes before he gave chase. He was doing this.' She paused, brow crinkled. 'Sir, how did you get here? How did you know what I'd done?'

Munce manoeuvred her onto the couch and took the seat beside her. 'We were following up on a tip from one of the homeless at Central. Said he'd seen a man watching female commuters in the week leading up to Holly's murder. This guy thought it was odd how the man always arrived and left in a courier van, even though he obviously wasn't working.'

He broke off and peered at the dead man. 'We found CCTV footage of this van, and when we did a trace of the plates, we came up with the name Benjamin Foster. Funniest thing, when DC Spencer spoke to the manager of the courier company, he mentioned another officer who'd asked him about that specific vehicle a few days earlier.'

Munce stopped and pinned Gina with his stare. She flinched but held his gaze.

'Of course, when Spencer came to me, it roused my suspicions, which were confirmed when I checked the log for the last time you accessed the database.'

'Oh,' she moaned.

'Oh, indeed. Once we discovered Benjamin Foster hadn't arrived home last night, despite his van being parked in the driveway, it wasn't a giant leap to suspect you were behind his disappearance.' Munce scratched his chin and cleared his throat. "Here's the thing; when we began investigating this Foster, the facts didn't line up, didn't make sense. Like the share house where he lived, not nearly private enough to commit murder without anyone seeing or hearing something. Not to mention his youth and level of education, which didn't match the sophisticated and intelligent killer we were hunting. We kept digging and found a link to another, a man fitting the profile, including his place of residence, secluded acreage in Mandalong Valley near Blackheath.'

Gina opened her mouth to ask a question, but before she could speak, the inspector answered it for her.

'The Homicide Squad despatched a team to the site hours ago and already I've received reports they've found evidence the women were killed in the homestead, before being driven to the base of the mountain and dumped.'

Munce paused and clasped her hand. 'Gina, if you'd spoken to me, confided what you were thinking, we could have worked together with all the resources of the force to track them, and apprehend them, the right way.'

Gina ignored his barb, her mind churning. 'What's his name, the killer?'

Munce nodded. 'Holden Stiles.'

'Holden Stiles,' Gina repeated in a soft voice, the act of naming the monster who'd pursued her through the garden making him human for the first time. 'JD,' she whispered. 'As in J. D. Salinger.'

When Munce peered at her with a puzzled expression, she explained. 'Sir, Benjamin kept calling the killer JD. He called himself that after the author who wrote *The Catcher in the Rye*, the protagonist of which is—'

'Holden Caulfield,' Munce finished for her.

Gina's brow crinkled. 'What did they find at his house?' she asked in a small voice.

The inspector opened a notepad he pulled from his jacket pocket. 'In the drawer of a bureau in the main bedroom, they found a wooden case in which lay a hypodermic, as well as a second compartment which was empty.'

Her hand fluttered to her neck where a gauze square covered the scratch mark where the needle had pierced her skin.

Munce glanced at her throat and nodded before returning his eyes to the page in front of him. 'Forensic collected hair samples from the pillows, believed to be from at least two different women, as well as skin scrapings.' He flipped the cover closed on his notebook and met Gina's eyes. 'They're still searching the property, and I suspect they'll find a lot more evidence tying Stiles to the murders.'

'Is he . . .' She gulped. 'Have they found him, sir?'

'Search and rescue located the body halfway down the gorge and are trying to retrieve it as we speak.' Munce brushed dirt from his jacket, his eyes never straying from her face.

He took her hands, the professional mask slipping as a tear formed at the corner of his eye. 'You might have died, Gina. What would I have told your father, your sisters?'

At the thought of her family, she moaned. She hadn't considered them when she made her plans, hadn't thought of anyone . . . except Tara.

'I take it Holden used Benjamin as a way of procuring the women,' Munce spoke, his words bringing Gina out of her torturous reverie.

'He was the collector,' she muttered, eyes on the dead boy. 'That's what he called himself. I suppose using such a sanitised title made it easier for him.'

'Did he tell you . . . Did he speak of Tara?' George asked in a reverent tone. He gulped, a single droplet quivering on his lashes.

Gina dipped her head, unable to speak for the lump lodged in her throat.

George swivelled to sit sideways on the couch cushion, facing her. 'What was the plan, Detective? What exactly were you going to do with this Benjamin?'

Gina's head dropped, a drumming starting in her ears. 'I wanted him dead.'

'Like this?' Munce said, pointing at the open wound at the young man's throat.

She started, head snapping back to meet his hooded eyes. 'No,' she replied, head shaking. 'I couldn't . . . not this.' Gina sighed, dropping her eyes to where her hands lay clenched in her lap. 'I was going to force him over the cliff edge like . . .'

'Like Holden,' Munce finished her sentence.

She fell silent as her mind flashed back to the moment she'd felt the man's hold on her ankle slip. 'I'm going to be sick.'

Gina teetered as her vision blurred, causing her to pitch forward. Munce leaped and caught her before she toppled onto Benjamin's body. She groaned, a hand clamped across her mouth. He led her from the sitting room, past the other officers, and into the bathroom.

She sank to the tiles beside the toilet. Her head hung over the bowl while bile splattered the porcelain. After the convulsions finished, she stood at the vanity, splashing water onto her face. She dried herself with a hand towel before examining her reflection. The woman staring back at her was a stranger.

They were her features: angular cheekbones, olive skin, full lips, and dark brows. It was the eyes which didn't belong to her. There was a haunted expression there, along with something else. She couldn't identify what it was, how it had altered her. She'd find out soon enough, she suspected, as she hobbled from the bathroom.

Munce was in the kitchen, his mobile against her ear. 'She's here now.' Without a word, he handed her the phone, which she stared at for a moment before bringing it to her ear.

'Hello,' she said in a small voice.

'Oh, Gina!' Akeisha exclaimed on the other end. 'Are you okay?'

'I'm fine, Keish. How's Bec? Is she all right?'

'She's better,' her friend replied. 'The doctor said she'll recover fully once the drug wears off and will be back to her usual self by morning.' There was a pause, and Gina's heart beat faster. 'Gee, what happened?'

She exhaled loudly into the phone, the skin of her neck and face flushed with guilt. 'I-I-I'm sorry,' she stammered. 'I didn't want to involve anyone, least of all you and Bec. Not after everything you've done for me.' Silence followed her words, and a sob lurched from her mouth.

'Shhh, I know you didn't,' Akeisha spoke in a tone reserved for a child. 'We'll talk later, when Bec's okay and we're home.'

'Thank you,' she mumbled, relief washing over her. She was too tired, too overwrought to explain herself. They ended the call with Gina assuring her friend she'd see them at the hospital. *If I'm not in handcuffs,* she thought to herself as she located Munce and handed the phone back to him.

'They ordered me to get you to rest,' he said with a half-smile. 'Your friend Greg here wants to take your vitals again.'

Gina hadn't noticed the handsome young man standing at Munce's side, and she considered him now. 'I'm fine,' she stated, to which he shook his head.

'You may feel okay,' he stated, eyebrows raised, 'but you still have a serious opiate in your bloodstream and until it leaves your system, I'm going to continue monitoring you.'

Gina cast an eye over her shoulder, looking for support from Munce, but he waved her away, and she had no choice but to let the paramedic lead her to the guest bedroom.

She ground her teeth as she lay on the bed while the paramedic took her pulse, checked her vision, and operated the blood-pressure armband. Her mind drifted as he talked of mundane things, his voice growing ever more distant as exhaustion grabbed at her, dragging her toward darkness.

K.J. STEWART

CHAPTER 33

GINA AWOKE TO ANOTHER beam of light in her eyes. She groaned and shook her head. This was becoming a habit.

'I'm sorry, Detective, but you can't sleep. Not yet,' Greg the paramedic spoke, his hand nudging her head until she met his gaze. 'I need you alert, okay? So, bear with me.'

'How long was I out?' she asked.

'Only a few minutes,' the man replied, the small torch piercing her retinas. 'Now let me do my thing.'

Just then, raised voices drifted through the half-open window. Something was happening in the garden. Gina pushed herself upright, shoving aside the medic's restraining hand.

One voice rose above the others. 'Inspector, you need to come quick. He's alive.'

Gina gritted her teeth and glared. 'I'm getting up, Greg, so don't try to stop me.'

The man opened his mouth to argue but instead held out his arm for support as she clambered out of bed. She pushed him away gently and staggered through the doorway into the lounge.

She couldn't see Munce, so she headed outside, taking a moment to wish she'd thrown on a heavy coat as the bitter night air wrapped around her. Her teeth clattered, and she burrowed her hands into the pockets of her hoodie.

Floodlights illuminated the bottom tier of the garden, where a gathering of uniforms huddled around something on the ground. Gina spotted Munce through the crowd.

'Gina!' a familiar voice called to her, and she turned to find her partner jostling others to reach her.

'Ravi!' she exclaimed, wrapping her arms around his neck and resting her head against his chest. She pulled away and glanced at his flushed face, his eyes avoiding hers.

He coughed, an expulsion to cover up his awkwardness. 'Are you okay?' he asked, head to one side as he studied her.

'Yes,' she said, eyes shifting to where the crowd huddled together. 'What's happening?'

'Search and rescue found this Holden Stiles,' Ravinder stated, eyes drilling into hers. 'Gina, he's still alive.'

'What?' she cried, her voice shrill. Her pulse thumped in her ears. How had he survived? It wasn't possible.

Gina threw herself into the crowd of officers, her partner after her. She shoved aside the onlookers to make her way to where Munce squatted next to an inert figure. A paramedic fitted an oxygen mask over the man's nose and mouth, while another inserted an intravenous drip into his arm.

Munce spotted her standing on the fringes of the clearing and approached her with a grim expression. 'Detective, I thought I told you to rest and let Greg take care of you,' he scolded. He sighed. 'I don't know why I bother. It's not as if anyone can stop you doing what you want.'

Gina held his stare, even while she flinched at his rebuke. 'Sir, what's his status?' she asked, eyes drifting to the unconscious man.

'He sustained severe spinal damage in the fall as well as a serious head injury.' Munce glanced over his shoulder at the man. 'They won't know the full extent until they get him to hospital and he's stable. If he survives that long.'

Gina flushed as a thought raced through her mind. *God, please don't let him live.* She cringed, remembering her orthodox upbringing and its emphasis on the sanctity of all life. *Not this one,* she railed.

'Everyone, stand back,' a paramedic ordered, the crowd shifting and breaking until they had cleared a path. Gina's heart flipped as the body

K.J. STEWART

on its stretcher passed her, and she got the first proper look at the man who'd killed Tara.

He was in his mid- to late thirties, she guessed, with straw-coloured hair he wore cropped to his scalp. His face was soft and squishy, with a heavyset brow and pale sideburns he wore wild and unkempt. The clothes he had on reminded her of a professor, and Gina recalled Benjamin mentioning his mother lectured at Sydney University. The stretcher moved past her, and she watched after him with a mixture of curiosity and revulsion.

Ravinder placed a hand on her shoulder. 'Let's get back inside before the inspector loses it and orders me to take you into custody.' Her partner escorted her back inside the cottage, where he sat her on the couch before draping a blanket across her shoulders. Even still, her body wouldn't stop shaking.

'Gina,' Munce said, appearing through the back doors, 'ring your father.'

She glanced at him, preparing to argue. It was too soon for her to talk to Anastasios, not while she remained shaken and addled. But when she met his determined gaze, she raised a hand to accept the phone he offered.

A moment later, her father's voice reached her. 'George, did you find her? Is Eugenia okay?'

Gina took a deep breath before answering. 'Papa, it's me.'

Stifled sobs filled her eardrum, and she held the phone away, an ache spreading through her chest.

'It's okay, Papa, I'm alright,' she blurted, her own tears spilling across her face.

'Eugenia, my girl!' Anastasios cried. 'Why do you risk yourself? We can't lose you after . . .' He broke off and wept harder, the unspoken name hanging between them: Tara.

'I'm sorry, Papa. Please forgive me,' she implored, now unable to see through the sheen of tears. 'I had to . . . It's just, I couldn't . . . Papa, I miss her so much, and I don't know how to continue . . .'

'Shhh, shhh, my Eugenia, it's okay. Everything is okay. You are safe. That is what matters for now.'

The deluge abated, and Gina hiccupped. 'I will see you soon, Papa, I promise. So don't worry. Okay, Papa? Don't worry for me.'

Gina realised the futility of her decree, but still, it seemed to calm her father, who asked to speak with George. She handed the phone to Munce and leaned against the couch cushion, drained and empty.

After a minute, the inspector cleared his throat, causing Gina's eyes to snap open, her vision blurred. It was exhaustion, not the drugs, she decided, head thumping. She'd give one of her kidneys for a solid twelve hours of sleep. *Maybe two days*, she decided, her mind struggling to focus on her superior's voice.

'Your personal carer, Greg, will take you to Nepean Hospital to get you checked over properly and for you to rest.' He raised a hand to stall her objection. 'You're no use here. Besides, you'll face difficult questions over the next day or two. I want you refreshed and prepared, no arguments.'

Gina dipped her head. He was right. The reality of her situation crouched on her chest. Besides, rest sounded good. She allowed Greg to escort her from the cottage into the back of a waiting ambulance. As the vehicle lumbered up the steep driveway, she kept her focus on the cottage. She recalled the last time she'd left it and shook her head at the similarities. Then, like now, her departure followed a violent death.

'I wish I could have saved you,' she whispered, an image of Sylvia dancing before her vision. The apparition beamed and nodded as if acknowledging her words and forgiving her failure.

By the time the ambulance pulled up at the emergency department, Gina as if she was sleepwalking. She barely noticed the nurses who ushered her into a ward, tucking her into a bed under layers of blankets. By the time the doctor had arrived, she struggled to keep her eyes open.

She passed the next hour in a fugue state as they prodded and probed all the tender bits of her. For now, she was almost thankful for the narcotic which held the worst of the aches at bay. When they finally pronounced it safe for her to sleep, she wondered how bad the pain would be when she awoke without any anaesthetic to dull it. It wasn't just the physical injuries she thought of as the darkness beckoned her into its warm embrace.

CHAPTER 34

'WHAT ARE YOU DOING here?' Munce asked, approaching where Gina sat outside the hospital room.

'I need to see him,' Gina replied with her chin lifted.

He took the seat beside her and patted her hand. 'You know you shouldn't be here, not while there's an investigation into your conduct underway.'

She shook her head, throat tight. 'I understand, sir, but I have to see him, to look into his face.' She withdrew her hand from under his.

Munce sighed and rubbed the bridge of his nose. He looked tired, as if he'd aged ten years in the fortnight since the events in Leura.

Upon waking in hospital, Gina had been overjoyed to find Bec and Akeisha at her bedside. The former was pale but okay. The three women had spoken of the man who'd drugged both Bec and Gina before the latter had led him over the edge of the cliff. Gina confessed to her friends how she'd 'borrowed' Akeisha's vehicle to abduct his accomplice, Benjamin. Their recriminations had been tepid, given their own fury and grief over the role he'd played in Tara's death.

Next, her father had arrived, accompanied by her sister Leda and her husband. 'Eugenia!' Anastasios had cried, scooping her into his tight embrace. 'Thank the good lord you are safe.'

Leda had wept salty tears against Gina's cheeks. 'You scared us half to death.'

The doctors had discharged her that day, and her family had bundled her into their car and taken her back to the apartment in Bondi. Gina couldn't think of it as hers now that Tara was no longer there. She realised she'd have to sell, but it was a decision for the future.

The days that followed had passed in a blur. She'd given her statement to a panel of senior officers, going over the details of how she'd tracked and kidnapped Benjamin and how she'd interrogated him. She'd left out details of her more robust tactics on Munce's advice, surprised when none of the officers questioned her as to his specific injuries. Gina suspected this was the inspector's doing and wondered how far in his debt she was.

As for the man who'd plunged into the gorge and survived, she'd stayed away as long as she could. But the compulsion to lay her eyes on him was too much, and here she was, metres from where he lay in an induced coma.

When she'd arrived an hour earlier, the officer stationed outside his room had refused her entry, and she assumed he was the one who'd contacted Munce.

'What's his condition?' she now asked the inspector, glancing toward the closed door.

He peered at her for a moment before answering. 'The fall fractured his spine in two places. If he were to recover, which he won't, he'd be paralysed.'

'Ha!' Gina exclaimed. 'Poetic.'

She averted her eyes when Munce stared at her from under a knit brow. A sigh hissed from between her tight lips when his head bobbed a moment later.

'The swelling on his brain is of greatest concern to the doctors. The damage is catastrophic, and he won't wake.'

She bowed her head till she was staring at her feet. 'Has he had any visitors, sir?'

Munce opened his mouth to answer when a commotion at the nurses' station drew his attention. A grey-haired woman was talking in a sharp voice, her tone and vestige domineering.

'Where's my son?' she demanded, eyes flashing at the hospital staff at the counter.

One pointed to the room in which Holden Stiles lay, and Gina and Munce shared a startled glance before focusing on the woman who'd birthed a killer.

Munce rose to his feet and approached the woman, who brushed aside the nurses with a dismissive gesture. She eyed the officer as he extended his hand toward her.

'I'm Detective Inspector Munce,' he stated, 'and I'm in charge of the investigation into your son's crimes.'

She peered at his hand, a sneer curling one side of her pressed lips. 'And are you also investigating the circumstances which brought him here?'

Munce let his hand fall to his side as he sized up the older woman. 'Mrs Stiles,' he began in a strained voice. 'Holden is under suspicion for the murder of three young women.'

'Humph,' she snorted, distaste clouding her features. 'He always was a worthless waste of oxygen.'

Gina watched the interchange, eyes on the woman who'd helped mould the monster her son became. She recalled Benjamin talking of how she'd ridiculed and belittled the young Holden, pitting him against the female sex from the outset.

The woman must have felt her stare because she faced Gina, one sculptured eyebrow raised. 'Who are you?' she asked in a haughty voice.

'Um, I'm Gina,' she replied, forcing herself to meet the icy stare. 'Detective Constable Palumbo.'

The older woman continued to stare, eyes narrowing to pinpoints of hatred and disdain. 'Yes,' she continued, dismissing her as beneath her notice, 'he was a pathetic creature from the beginning. His father took off when Holden was a child, leaving me to raise the cowering, snivelling child. I should have sent the boy to him years ago. Maybe he'd have made a man of him. But as it was, the job of managing Holden fell on me.'

Gina stared at her, mouth agape. To speak of her own child this way sent ice through her veins. For a moment, she pitied the man lying in a coma. The woman's words formed a sombre and disturbing picture of his childhood, despised and reviled by his own mother.

'God knows I tried to make him a man, to toughen him up,' Holden's mother continued. 'I enrolled him in sports, but he was hopeless at everything. Not to mention he whined and cried before every game. Such a scared little ninny, afraid of the dark, jumping at shadows. I tried to get him to face his fears with plenty of time out in the basement, but he was beyond help.'

'Jesus,' Gina whispered under her breath, wincing when she felt the weight of the woman's iron stare on her.

'Don't judge me, young lady,' she ordered. 'You cannot countenance what it was to raise such a pansy.'

Gina could take it no longer. She rose to her feet and pushed her shoulders back and jaw forward. 'What of your own responsibility?' she asked in a controlled voice, even as pounding blood filled her eardrums. 'He killed those women after you drummed into him how he wasn't good enough. Not for the girls you taught, not even for his own mother.'

She sucked in her breath. The venom in the woman's expression chilled Gina's blood and set her heart tripping. Still, she held her stare, refusing to cower and relent beneath it.

'How do you know this?' the older woman asked.

Gina caught Munce shaking his head from the corner of her eye and bit her tongue. She inhaled deeply, exhaling in a hiss. 'Your son killed women after you told him over and over he wasn't worthy of their attention. They were people with families, loved ones.'

The woman stared, eyes reflecting no emotion. 'This is nothing to me.'

'Nothing to you,' Gina repeated, brain screaming and mouth gaping. 'He killed my fiancée, you subhuman wretch.'

The expression on the older lady's face shifted. Her nose crinkled as if a foul odour had filled the room, and her lips pressed into a thin red line. 'The way I see it, dear, it's one less abomination in the world.'

Red-hot fury swelled through Gina's innards, and her fists clenched. It had been a long time since she'd heard such overt hatred directed toward her for her sexuality.

Just as her anger threatened to explode, a man in a white coat rounded the corner. 'You must be Mrs Stiles,' he stated, glancing between them before settling on the grey-haired woman.

'Roberta,' the woman spoke in a sweet voice, holding out her hand for him to clasp.

Gina's mind reeled at the change in her demeanour, the way her personality altered when the doctor appeared. Disgust filled her pores while nausea gripped her stomach.

Meanwhile, Munce introduced himself. 'What's the prognosis, Doc?' he asked, his eyes catching Gina's while a slight shake of his head cautioned her silence.

The doctor glanced at Gina before facing Mrs Stiles. 'I'm sorry to inform you, but your son's injuries are too catastrophic for him to recover. Holden's brain shows no signs of activity, and the machines are keeping him alive. Without them, he cannot sustain life. I recommend—'

'Turn them off,' the woman interrupted, her words drawing a look of shock from the doctor, whose eyes flicked between Munce and Gina.

The inspector shrugged, while Gina shook her head, her stare on the callous woman who was fishing in her purse for something. A moment later, she drew out a mobile phone and glanced at the screen.

'I have to run,' she announced as if she was at a social gathering instead of discussing her son's impending demise.

The doctor's mouth gaped, and his head tilted. 'Don't you want to say goodbye, stay with him?'

Mrs Stiles met his eyes, a grimace flitting across her face. 'No, Doctor. I have a lecture to prepare and papers to mark. Just do it and then send me the bill.' She offered him her hand, which he took after a moment's hesitation.

'As you wish,' he said in a stilted tone, releasing her and rubbing his palm against his coat as if trying to wipe the heartlessness from it. 'I'll ask you to please sign the consent form before you leave.'

Mrs Stiles took the pen he offered, scrawling her signature onto a form she didn't bother reading. With one last glance between Munce and Gina, she pivoted on her expensive heels and strode along the corridor. The group stared after her until she disappeared.

'Right,' the doctor exclaimed, his expression bewildered.

'Charming,' Munce said in a deadpan voice. 'Very maternal.'

Gina couldn't speak; so shocked was she by the woman's indifference toward her son, his crimes, and his imminent death. Again, pity for Holden coursed through her. She shook her head.

'What happens now?' Munce asked the doctor, who still appeared shell-shocked.

'Yes,' he said, shaking his head and meeting the inspector's eyes. 'We will switch off the machines and have a nurse sit with the patient until he passes.'

'I'll do it,' Gina volunteered before she'd even thought on it. She glanced at Munce, who squinted, absorbing her expression.

'I'll stay too,' he announced, sending a wave of relief through Gina. She didn't know why she'd volunteered to sit with the man who'd murdered her lover. But even as she pondered this, she realised it was what Tara would have done if it was she who'd died.

A gentle peace settled across her chest, and she nodded at Munce, who returned the gesture, motioning for her to enter the room first.

Gina held her breath as she neared the hospital bed. Holden Stiles lay motionless – abused and neglected child, murderer, and torturer of women. There were tubes running from several points of his thin frame, and the noises from the machines they fed into filled the otherwise silent space.

She exhaled a burst of air, her hand shaking as she lifted it toward Holden Stiles. She paused, her fingers centimetres from his face and tears stinging her eyes.

'You took my love, my heart and future,' she said, bitterness twisting her guts. She breathed in and out, her thoughts filled with Tara. She leaned forward until her mouth hovered above his ear. 'I'm sorry you had such a dreadful childhood,' she whispered. 'Now rot in hell,' she added before standing upright and taking a step away from the bed to allow the doctor passage.

Gina stood beside Munce while he made a last examination before removing the mask covering the patient's airways. He then moved to the machines and flicked switches until silence blanketed the room. The heart monitor continued to display its curves and lines that measured the life left in the comatose man.

The doctor retreated from the room, leaving Munce and Gina alone with a nurse who stood on the other side of the bed, her fingers resting on the pulse at Holden's wrist.

K.J. STEWART

Minutes ticked by, the patient's rasping, straining breathing replacing the machine's pips. Gina became aware of George clasping her hand without remembering when he'd taken it.

'How long, nurse?' he asked.

The nurse shook her head. 'It differs, although his pulse is thready and erratic, so it won't be long.'

The two officers stood together in silence, each glancing between the man's face and the monitor which showed his heart slowing its pumping, the spikes and dips growing smaller until they disappeared, replaced by a single straight line. A strangulated hiss of air passed between his lips before his chest fell and silence filled the room.

The nurse placed a stethoscope to the man's chest before glancing at her wristwatch. 'Time of death, 10:38 a.m.'

Holden's story was at an end.

CHAPTER 35

'THE BOARD HAS READ your statement and have examined the evidence submitted in this disciplinary case.'

Gina didn't recognise the officer heading the panel and her mind consumed with what she had to do, had forgotten his name. There were four senior officers, including Munce, seated behind a long table, while Gina sat in a chair facing them. She felt like a prisoner awaiting sentence, which, in a way, she was.

'While we have decided not to press criminal charges, Detective Palumbo, your decision to work outside of law enforcement has brought into question your suitability as a police officer,' the man stated with an inscrutable expression.

Gina nodded, heart thumping. 'Yes, sir,' she stated in a controlled voice. She knew what she had to do, but still, she hesitated.

'Do you deny you abducted a suspect in an ongoing murder investigation?'

This was it, the moment she had to speak. 'Yes, sir. I mean, no, sir, I don't.'

Before she could continue, he spoke again after glancing toward Munce. 'While we appreciate the extraordinary circumstances which led to this flagrant indiscretion and flaunting of protocol, we cannot allow our officers to turn vigilante – regardless of the provocation.'

Gina nodded, bitterness filling her throat. 'With all due respect, sir . . . sirs,' she said, her gaze sweeping along the panel, 'but you speak of circumstances and provocation. Let's talk plainly. This Holden Stiles, with the assistance of his loyal collector, Benjamin, murdered the love of my life . . . in a sick and twisted way. She'd have seen her death coming while being powerless to prevent it.'

She broke off as a sob threatened to erupt from her throat. Gina gulped, raising a hand when the man frowned and opened his mouth to speak.

'But that's neither here nor there,' she stated in a weary voice. 'I'm resigning from the force, effective immediately.'

A stunned silence fell across the room, and Gina's eyes searched out Munce, whose expression reflected sadness but not shock. She realised he'd anticipated her decision.

'I can no longer perform the duties of an officer of the law,' she said. 'I went too far down the rabbit hole to come back to the job. I offer my unreserved apology for putting the force and any colleagues or superiors in jeopardy. That was not my intention, and I'm sorry for any fallout my actions have caused.'

The silence continued, broken by panel members shifting in their chairs and clearing their throats. The head of the panel cast his eyes from one side of the line to the other, and Gina noted the various members nodding, the last of which was Munce.

'While we regret losing such a promising officer, we accept your resignation and believe it to be the best outcome . . . for everyone.' He banged the gavel in his right hand.

The panel broke apart, its members exiting the room, some without acknowledging Gina, while others shook her hand as they passed.

'Well,' Munce exclaimed when only they remained, 'that's that then.'

'I'm sorry, George,' Gina said, eyes filling with tears. 'I didn't mean to cause you trouble. I hope I haven't damaged your reputation or career.'

Munce stepped forward and hugged her, his arms squeezing her until she grunted, and he released her. 'Nonsense,' he said, his own eyes shimmering. 'Nothing I can't handle. Don't spend another minute worrying for me.'

They remained lost in their own thoughts.

'What now?' he asked finally in a strained voice.

Gina shrugged. 'I don't know. I know little anymore. Except that ever since Tara died, there's a gaping hole in me that the job won't fill.' She fell into silence, contemplating her next words. 'I'm lost, George. I don't understand who I am without her, and until I work that out, I'm no use to anyone . . . least of all myself,' she said with a tired laugh.

He patted her shoulder. 'Well, remember, I'm here for you, and if there's something I can do to help, any support I can give, you need only ask.'

Gina couldn't speak, not without dissolving into tears, something she'd done so often in front of the inspector that she couldn't bear it again. Instead, she nestled against his chest while his arms clasped her to him.

In the car on the way home, Gina smiled. A weight lifted from her chest, and she could breathe again. She'd done it. As difficult as it was to leave her partner, her colleagues, and especially Munce, she'd severed ties to her old life.

The relief dissipated as shame flushed her skin. She cringed as she recalled her words to Munce when he had asked her what came next. 'I don't know,' she'd replied. It was bullshit, a contrived response.

She knew exactly what she intended to do. It was a plan which began in Sylvia's cottage when she had found Freya's diary. Her thirst for justice remained unsated, and while it pained her to have to lie, it was necessary. She hadn't lied when she told the panel she was too far down the rabbit hole. The part she'd omitted was she had no intention of returning topside. At least, not yet.

Munce couldn't know of the next stage of her life. No one could. She was alone but for the Tara who lived in her heart and memories. While she had no illusions of what her dead lover would say of her intentions, she'd stand by Gina's side and support her every step of the way.

She smiled as she pulled into the underground car park at their apartment. 'For you, my love. For all those lost to human evil.' It was her new mantra.

K.J. STEWART

EPILOGUE

S UNLIGHT BEAT UPON THE bronze plaque, glinting off the letters etched across it. Since there were no remains as such, Tara's family had bought a plot of earth at Rookwood Cemetery, where they'd placed a plaque for loved ones to visit. Gina was glad.

Trees and well-maintained lawn surrounded the area in which she sat. There was a stone bench nearby, which Gina ignored, preferring instead to sit on the grass in front of the plaque, her eyes running over the epitaph.

'I've sold the apartment,' she announced, flicking a wind-flung strand of hair from her lips. 'It feels strange, but I got a good price for it; enough to finance my temporary move.' Gina's fingers stroked the hard surface of the plaque. 'I know you may not approve,' she whispered, 'but I think you'd understand.'

Her voice broke as grief raced along her gullet. 'I don't know who I am without you, T. It's like I can feel you with me, beside me. But when I reach for you, there's nothing but air.' She groaned as agony clawed at her insides.

'Fuck, T, how am I supposed to go on without you? I can hear your voice in my ear. "Gina, baby, you're strong and courageous, and you'll go on fine without me," you say, as if it's that easy. What if I don't?' she wailed, anger slicing through her grief. 'What if I throw in the towel, give up on this life of misery, injustice, and evil?'

Even as the words gushed from her mouth, the image of her family and friends raced through her mind. *Stop with the theatrics,* she scolded herself. Of course, she had no intention of taking her own life. As impossible as it was to see the path ahead, she wouldn't quit. Not while her mission propelled her.

This last thought prompted her to fish inside her bag, pulling out a leather-bound diary, which she placed on her lap.

Gina closed her eyes, the sun warming her face. With a deep sigh, she opened at the page she'd marked back at Sylvia's cottage and began to read.

> When I told Sylvia my story all those years ago on the train to Sydney, I omitted one important detail. I wanted to tell her but couldn't bring myself to speak of it. Perhaps I'll yet find the courage.
>
> It relates to those nights spent in the basement at the house in Toorak. You see, it wasn't only my father who had abused me and my sister, something I never told my dearest friend. Sylvia believed I had just the one sibling, my sister and fellow victim. But there was also Nathaniel. He was three years my sister's senior, the eldest child and the apple of our parents' eyes.
>
> When Nathaniel turned 15, my father initiated him into his special club. I have no way of knowing if he tried to refuse hiss twisted legacy, but it doesn't matter in the end.
>
> The most unbearable truth is that our own brother enjoyed our young bodies. Not only that, he reaped the profits that came from passing us around as playthings.

There was more, but Gina raised her eyes from the page, her gaze fiery steel. When she'd found the diary, her hope was that Freya's father still lived, even while she realised this was impossible. He'd be long dead, having escaped punishment for his heinous crimes against his own flesh and blood.

Then she'd come to this part, and a plan formed in her mind. There was yet someone to hold to account, a person deserving of the fists of justice – her fists. She rubbed the skin of her knuckles, still bearing faint scars from pummelling Benjamin.

She brought her focus back to Tara's plaque, the words gleaming against the bronze.

> Tara Louise Bennett, beloved daughter and sister.
> Forever in our hearts and minds. Rest in peace, angel.

She brushed the tips of her fingers across her lips before pressing them to her lover's name. With a groan, she rose to her feet, shaking first one foot and then the other, wincing as the blood tingled through her extremities.

'I don't know how long I'll be gone, but I promise to visit when I return. Remember, I love you always,' she added before forcing herself to pirouette and walk away on stiff legs.

As she strode through the cemetery toward her car, she smiled grimly. The hole in her gaped, its edges shredded. She was incomplete, a chunk of her empty, missing. But she had a path going forward.

Not for the first time, a line of the poem Tara's patient had written floated into her mind. 'Ink bleeds into blackened ends, twisting regard, come eternal penned.' She found herself wondering whether the poet had found help elsewhere, hoping he wasn't floundering alone without Tara as she was.

So be it, she mused, tipping her head. A captive in her own story of grief and loss she might be, but she'd set fire to its pages and burn all the jailers with it.

For all those lost to human evil, she'd make them pay.